Marked by Fire

Sons of Britain #1

MIA WEST

MARKED BY FIRE

Copyright © 2017 Mia West

Cover Design © 2016 Mia West

Cover Images © sergiophoto | Shutterstock

All rights reserved.

ISBN-13: 9781549525711

Edition Note: This title was originally published in 2016 as a novella. The author has significantly expanded the story for republication as a novel.

DEDICATION

For everyone who's ever been young and stupid

CHAPTER 1

Northern Cymru, 515 CE

Arthur stared at the man across the fire and wondered what would happen if the uninked son of a healer and a blacksmith pulled a warlord's heir into a dark corner and told him he wanted to fuck.

He'd get his jaw cracked, if he was lucky. Dragged back into the firelight and shamed, if less fortunate.

Arthur rubbed his jaw. There would be no confessing, in the dark or the light. Besides, Bedwyr was his older brother's closest friend and shieldmate. If Cai found out…

He spotted his brother not far away, arms crossed smugly, sleeves rolled up as always to show off his ink. Others sometimes remarked how much Cai resembled their father, but beyond his hair and height Arthur didn't see it. Where their father was humble, Cai boasted. Where Matthias chose his words with care and consideration, Cai acted on his first instinct. Fine for the battlefield, Arthur supposed, but he'd felt the brunt of it enough times to know the instinct usually only served Cai and his pride.

No, Arthur had contented himself with watching Bedwyr for years—every one of his eighteen, it seemed sometimes. That would have to be enough, and just now, at the coldest, snowiest part of the year in Cymru, he had little else to do.

The village was gathered in the meeting hall for the evening story fire. While Tiro, their resident storyteller, got ready to continue the tale he'd begun a few nights before, people milled about, laughing and jesting and generally trying to hold off the gloom of midwinter. Light from the central pit flickered over their faces, turning smiles into grimaces and back again. Children ran about, shrieking, chased by a couple of shaggy hounds.

Arthur shifted on his bench and studied Bedwyr over the rim of his mug. Bedwyr sat next to his father, as usual. Lord Uthyr's raised chair boasted a high back covered in furs. He lounged in it, a horn of drink in one hand. Bedwyr shared Uthyr's black hair, his bull-like frame, and, by all accounts, his single-minded fierceness in battle—Cai had told Arthur stories that had raised the small hairs on his arms. If he were honest, half the reason he wanted to fight among the other warriors was to see Bedwyr in his element. Just imagining it had, on countless nights, sent him off to sleep tangled in sticky blankets.

It was widely expected that Bedwyr would succeed Uthyr when the lord could no longer lead men. Such a scenario seemed unlikely anytime soon, and no one said such a thing aloud, let alone where Uthyr might hear them. Any compliment paid to Bedwyr was immediately credited to Uthyr's stock and training of him.

As ferocious as he might be in a skirmish, Bedwyr always sat just so in the evenings: quietly as his neighbors bustled about. When Arthur was a boy at his lessons, Master Philip had told him that their world and others in the night sky circled the sun, as if each were a stone in a great sling. The old man was wise, but Arthur doubted that particular bit of lore—a product, maybe, of Philip's longtime partnership with Tiro, master of tall tales. The sun clearly arced over the earth, east to west, as did the moon and stars.

In that way Bedwyr was like the earth: solid and reliable, unperturbed by everything and everyone around him. Just now his dark eyes were trained on the fire. He had thick lashes, thicker even than his sister Gwen's. His boots were planted wide before him, forearms resting on knees, big hands loose and relaxed. His shirt hid his ink, which Arthur only saw on occasions when the training men cooled off with a swim in a pond, or when Bedwyr sat for new ink following a skirmish. He bore dragons, the sign of his father's house, one on each arm. The rest of his tattoos were confined to his chest and belly, almost invisible under the hair there. Arthur's fingers itched with wanting to trace their shapes.

He curled his hands into fists, lest Bedwyr sense them. But

Bedwyr only watched the fire calmly, his face betraying nothing of his thoughts.

Then another face was there—Eira, Uthyr's latest companion. After a few whispered words, she drew back, smiling as Bedwyr rose to join her. They disappeared through the rug hanging at the rear of the hall.

Arthur looked away, the futility of his want threatening to crush him. He would never have Bedwyr, let alone get to touch him outside of pounding on each other with sword and shield in the training yard. And if this fucking winter didn't end, he'd never fight either.

Restless, he stood and paced about the hall. He nodded to his parents, who, as usual, sat against the wall, listening to Tiro. Master Philip sat next to them, a fond smile on his lined face as he watched his partner entertain the village. Arthur almost tripped on the foot set in his path by his twelve-year-old sister, Mora, avoiding it only because he'd turned away from the contentment on Philip's face.

He needed air.

The dark chill outside welcomed him, cooling his burning cheeks. He took in a great breath, blowing it out in a long, steamy cloud. Stars glittered overhead as he turned down the side of the building. Shuffling through the snow, he made for the back corner and the shed built there to store the building's firewood. It would be quiet. He could think—better yet, *not* think. Just sit amid the comforting spice of cut wood and breathe. He had rounded the edge of the lean-to before he heard the unmistakable sounds of sex.

Or, well, half the sounds. In the dim light provided by a crescent moon, he made out Bedwyr sitting on a low stack of firewood. His trousers lay puddled around his boots. Eira knelt between his splayed knees, her head bobbing, her hand jerking hard. The noises that rose in the quiet space came from her, appreciative hums and the slurping sounds of her labors.

Bedwyr was silent.

Arthur watched him, fascinated. He didn't want a woman, but he knew himself well enough to know that if one had pinned him down and swallowed his cock, he would have made some noise.

But Bedwyr only sat on the woodpile, his hands gripping the sawn edges of the logs. He seemed to be staring at something on the ground past Eira's shoulder.

Then his eyes flashed up and caught Arthur spying.

He felt like a young buck, trapped between a bear and a boulder, no antlers yet to defend himself. He should step away. Now. He should go. *Now*.

Bedwyr's lips parted as if he would speak, and Arthur blurted, "Had to piss."

Eira lifted her head with a slick *pop* and turned to gape at him. After a few seconds, she began to laugh.

Arthur bolted.

Back in the hall, he tried to lose himself in Tiro's tale, but he mostly heard the erratic thump of his own heartbeat. He shouldn't have come inside. He should have gone back to his family's house on the edge of the village. Eira would finish her work, and then he'd have to see that satisfaction on Bedwyr. Most people probably couldn't, but he'd spent so many years studying Bedwyr's face, his posture, his every fucking move, that he would see it. *Had* seen it. This wasn't the first time one of Uthyr's women had led his son from the hall.

Arthur grabbed a cup of ale and tipped it high.

~ ~ ~

Bedwyr stared at the empty space where the cub had stood. Moonlight slashed into the woodshed now as if no one had thrown a shadow only moments before. The snow in the doorway was scuffed, and he recalled how the quick turn of Arthur's boots had sent a small spray of it glittering. The long queue of his hair had been the last thing to disappear from sight.

Eira purred in his lap, drawing his attention back to her moments before her small, bony hand took hold again, choking his cock. He shifted, trying to ignore the rising sense of panic he nearly always felt in this situation.

But everyone expected this of him. From the time he'd been a boy, whether training him or disciplining him, or even just sharing a joke, his father had only ever handled him roughly. And his father's women...from the first one Uthyr had insisted he enjoy, their hands had moved on him as if he were made of stone, or fired clay. He was the warlord's son. How else should he be handled? How else could he possibly want it done? They had asked him, of course—he was Uthyr's son and could have had them any way he pleased.

He'd never been able to admit what he truly wanted. He'd had only to imagine the resulting cast to their expressions: pity that he couldn't take it rough, or contempt that he craved a softer caress. Let alone that he'd wished them all to be men.

The only thing for it, he'd found, was to make himself grow as blood-hard as possible, and so he did now what he always did. Closed his eyes and imagined the man. Tall and broad-shouldered. Long hair the color of winter grass, tied neatly behind him, his beard a shade darker and beginning to show silver. Eyes whose brown would be muted in this dark, and downcast besides. A mouth that smiled often when he wasn't speaking soft, inquiring words. Large hands that had only ever touched Bedwyr gently, in life and in these fantasies he'd never admit to.

When the shadow had crept into his line of sight moments before, it had been long enough that Bedwyr's belly had iced over, thinking the man himself had caught him at one of these furtive, useless interludes. But as tall as Arthur was, he hadn't quite reached his father's height, or the calm stillness Matthias seemed to exhibit at any given moment.

Bedwyr was a fool. He knew this. Matthias was content in his marriage, thoroughly suited to his wife. He was their healer. The health of every person in the village was Matthias's domain and vocation. He'd never given Bedwyr any reason to believe his kindness held an interest beyond looking after his well-being. Bedwyr was probably the only one to have twisted the man's voice and touch to his own private use. He imagined them now, settling over him like a lamb's-wool blanket, imagined blood pulsing into his cock, making it heavy and rendering him as hard as everyone thought him to be.

It didn't work. No amount of will seemed to muffle Eira's squeals or equal the clutching grip of her hand. He grabbed her wrist to still it.

She looked up. "Harder?"

Gods' blood. "No." He removed her hand from him.

"You want to fuck me? You can, you know. Your father doesn't mind—"

"No." He mashed himself back into his breeches and jerked at the laces. "Not tonight."

Not ever, if he could help it.

Eira rose with a sour expression. "Idiot boy."

He looked at her, surprised. None of them had ever gone that far, even when he'd deserved it. But she was glaring at the empty doorway. She was talking about Arthur.

"Who skulks about on a winter night?" she grumbled.

"We did."

"I don't skulk. I serve my lord." She swatted at her skirts. "If Cai's brother had a woman of his own, he wouldn't have to spy on you."

"He wasn't spying," Bedwyr said, feeling testy. "And he's no idiot."

"Could have fooled me."

Probably.

He opened the rear door of the hall and gestured her to go ahead of him. Once she had, shoulders straightened and chin high, he found he didn't want to follow her inside. Closing the door behind her, he left the lean-to the same way Arthur had gone.

Stars shone overhead, the dragon to the north, the great bear to its right. He should have just come outside to watch them when he'd grown bored. As he walked the length of the outer wall, he wondered if Arthur had stepped out to do the same. Winters were long and wearisome, with little to do but train for the following spring. Judging by the number of babes born in late summer and early autumn, his neighbors spent a fair number of these dark hours warming their beds. His own bed was no refuge from boredom, except by his own hand, and it was likely to remain so.

Quick footfalls drew his attention to the road. A few seconds later Gwilym, one of their scouts, ran past. Bedwyr hurried after. By the time he entered the hall, it was in an uproar, men shouting and women bustling about. He walked toward his father's chair, intent on hearing it plain. Halfway there, a man stepped into his path, colliding with him.

Arthur took a hasty step back. Color rode high on his cheeks, and he stared at Bedwyr, his mouth open but saying nothing. This close, Bedwyr had to look up to meet his eyes.

"What's happened?" he asked.

Arthur swallowed. "Saxons."

Hail the gods.

The lookouts had spotted them by the trail of smoke they'd left in their path. A small band, but far enough into Cymru to be a threat. Winter or no, there would be a fight.

"We'll put them down handily," Uthyr said. "They don't know these mountains as we Cymry do, and the snow won't make it any easier for them." He gave them his wolfish grin. "You'll be back in your own beds, fucking your fine women, within the week."

The fighting men cheered at that. Bedwyr made himself shout with them, then moved closer to his father for orders. He received a nod, but then Uthyr called to Arthur. The lad approached, looking as if he was bracing himself. When Arthur stood before him, Uthyr gripped the back of his neck and drew him close.

"Find a cunt and fill it," Uthyr said. "Takes the edge off."

Arthur looked back intently. "I'm to fight?"

Bedwyr's father chuckled. "You're to fight."

The cub seemed coiled to spring into the rafters. He gave a curt nod. "Thank you, my lord."

Cai appeared behind Arthur and gave his shoulders a rough shake. "Maybe you'll finally get a woman, little brother."

A familiar look of annoyance crossed Arthur's face as he pulled away from Cai. "Leave off."

By all accounts—and several circulated about the village—Arthur was a virgin. Though he'd been served by several, Bedwyr had never fucked a woman, either. He wondered what the cub's excuse was. A single-minded focus on earning his first tattoo, if he had to guess.

As if reading his mind, Cai said, "At least Dafydd will finally ink over that thing on your arm."

Arthur's gaze flicked to Bedwyr but too quickly to read. Then he pushed past Cai, jostling him. "Fuck you."

"Thanks, no," Cai called after his brother. "I have other options."

Cai was his shieldmate and closest friend. Didn't mean he wasn't also a goat's arsehole. He'd long ago worked his way through the willing women in their village. "Your right hand, you mean."

Cai waved him off, unoffended. "I'd give it for a good fight."

"Tempt the gods, why don't you?"

"I'll thank them for Saxon stupidity." Cai hunched his shoulders, then gave Bedwyr's a punch. "Midwinter treat, eh?"

On that he agreed. Winter in the lowlands of Britain must be unbearable to make the dogs think Cymru's mountains would be more hospitable.

He would send them fleeing, tails docked as a warning to the rest.

CHAPTER 2

Bedwyr woke to a heavy hand at his throat. He jerked his dagger upward, only to find his wrist caught in an unrelenting hold.

His father crouched above him, eyes like black stones. "Passable," he said. "Get up." Then he rose and walked away.

Bedwyr sat up. Extricating his boots from the blankets took some doing; as usual, he'd kicked hard at his father's choking grip. At least he hadn't pissed himself. He had done, once, at home. His father hadn't shamed him for it, had only told him to master himself. A panicked bladder signaled an unfocused mind.

Willing his pulse to settle, he glanced around the camp, wondering if anyone had witnessed the morning ritual. Men were up and moving, but if any of them had seen it, none let on.

Except for Arthur. He was staring after Uthyr with something between awe and terror. When his gaze slid across the cold fire pit to meet Bedwyr's, he blinked, his eyes wide.

Bedwyr began to gather his gear. He could say something to the lad, something reassuring. Not about the hand to the throat but the work of the day ahead. It would be Arthur's first skirmish. Uthyr had made him wait for it, work for it, longer than anyone Bedwyr could remember. And Arthur had: he trained every waking moment he wasn't eating. He was strong, with an enviable height—taller even than Cai—yet quick despite it. Bedwyr figured he wasn't the only warrior who looked forward to seeing what Arthur would bring to a fight.

But he was reckless. He wanted too badly to prove himself, to impress Uthyr ap Emrys, warlord and Pen y Ddraig. Bedwyr's father had assigned Huw to be shieldmate to Arthur today. The man had grunted his assent without further comment—every veteran took his turn protecting the new fighters from themselves. Huw had done the same for Bedwyr, and Tiro for Cai.

As far as Bedwyr was concerned, that should have been the end of it. He should put the matter of Arthur's greenness out of his mind and spend his hours preparing for his own work. They would find the Saxons today. He would fight alongside Cai, as he had for the three years since his father deemed them ready to shield each other. They worked well as a unit, had trained together under Cai's grandfather, Marcus Roman.

But that was the problem: their teamwork was instinct now. Even at this moment, they moved in tandem, packing their bedding and arming themselves, no words required. It left too much room to think.

"You should say something to him."

Cai glanced up. "Who?"

Bedwyr cocked his chin to where Arthur packed his own gear, alone.

"He'll be fine," Cai said. "Huw will mind him."

"Still. Something."

"You're such a nursemaid."

"Fuck you."

"Why does everyone say that to me?"

Bedwyr gave him a wry look.

Cai sighed. "Fine. I'll say something."

"Don't be an arse about it."

Cai made a rude gesture and crossed the camp to where his brother was strapping on a sword belt. Bedwyr watched surreptitiously as Arthur listened to Cai. The skin of his face, usually ruddy as any other redhead's, looked as slick and pale as a cooked egg white. It made the freckles stand out, as if he'd been spattered with mud. Or blood. Could be he'd wear both before the day ended.

Arthur nodded at whatever Cai said, then turned away.

Cai walked back to Bedwyr, smirking. "Happy, mother hen?"

Content enough.

He turned his mind away from green lads and toward the fight ahead.

~ ~ ~

Arthur felt like vomiting.

His father had offered him herbs on his departure with the war party, but no one else took such things, so he'd refused them. He was already the youngest of the men, the only one among them without the tattoo that would mark him a warrior of his people. That is, if he didn't count the tattoo he'd given himself at ten. (He didn't.) The last thing he needed was to be seen accepting a comfort remedy like a suckling babe.

He hadn't been able to avoid his father's embrace—Matthias ap Marcus still had an inch on him. He'd suffered the hug under his older brother's smirk.

At least his mother hadn't embarrassed him. She'd stood back, her blacksmith's apron already tied on, hammer at her belt. She'd only nodded to him, jaw set, before turning for her workshop.

That had been three days before. Lord Uthyr had led their band of forty southeast across the mountains. With frequent reports from the scouts, they found the Saxons in a valley between two passes. The invaders numbered about twenty—enough to harass a small village but not so many they couldn't be overcome. Cymru's mountains were still foreign to them. *Flatlanders,* Uthyr called them with a sneer. Chances were, he'd said, the invaders would run at the first threat.

Arthur silently willed them to stay and fight.

Under cover of the trees on either side of the path, they surrounded the Saxon band. They were a rough-looking pack of dogs, their clothing unsuited to the cold and snow. Most huddled about low-burning campfires, with a few stomping about as if to warm their feet. As a whole they looked bone-chilled and scrawny, but at that thought Arthur reminded himself that his grandfather Marcus, while taller than most in the village, had been wiry. It had rendered him quick and agile, and Arthur had never bested him in the training yard.

Huw tipped his head silently, gesturing for Arthur to kneel beside him. Snow melted through his trousers almost immediately, chilling his knee. It sent a shiver up his spine, exacerbating his need to piss. There was nothing for it now—who knew when Uthyr would give the signal. He flexed his fingers and renewed his grip on his sword.

The rim of his shield rested on the ground. He rolled his shoulders while he could.

"You'll be fine, lad. Follow my lead."

Huw's profile looked hard as ever, and blunt where a long-ago blade had taken the tip of his nose.

"And when I say *follow*," Huw muttered, "I mean stay behind me."

Ha. Not likely. If he wasn't one of the first to the fight, there wouldn't be a Saxon to be had.

He glanced down the line of men crouching among the trees. Cai was there, several shields down, his eyes on the valley, a muscle ticking in his jaw. Just beyond him knelt Bedwyr.

Their trek to this place had given him three days and nights to watch Bedwyr and how he might be different away from the village. In some ways, he was—more given to joking and laughing, and talking in general. Two nights in, he told a story Arthur had never heard before, about the stars in the northern sky. When Bedwyr was a lad, before his father had decided his lessons with Master Philip were sufficient, the constellations had marked the only time Bedwyr had argued with the cleric. After all, Master Philip insisted on calling the dragon Draco, when every man in Cymru knew it was the *ddraig*. When Philip had told him the civilized Romans had called the great bear next to it Ursa, Bedwyr had shouted that that was the *arth* and Romans should have minded their empire instead of giving the stars stupid names.

Arthur couldn't imagine Bedwyr having such an outburst, and he'd laughed along with everyone else. Unfortunately the tale had prodded Cai to dredge up Arthur's old nickname—cub—and they'd all had a good chuckle at Arthur's expense. Would he bring his teeth and claws to the Saxons, or would he trundle off to some cave to doze away the winter instead?

It had taken everything Arthur had not to snarl at Cai; that would only have made it worse. He'd said only that he'd go for the invaders' throats and let the gods judge his worth.

Cai had waved off his bravado, as Cai always did. But Bedwyr had held Arthur's eye and nodded. Only later, when he lay in his bedroll recalling that nod, did he wonder if Bedwyr had told the bear story on purpose, as some sort of initiation. If so, Arthur had passed it, at least in one man's mind.

Now, as they waited to attack, Bedwyr was so still he could have been hewn from stone. Gone was any hint of a smile. His brow was locked down, his focus total. He was choosing his first opponent—Cai said Bedwyr did that before every skirmish. So far, none had survived.

Somewhere in the valley walked a man who had better be right with his gods.

Suddenly Bedwyr surged up, his mouth open on a shout, and Arthur jolted, realizing Uthyr's sharp whistle had just pierced the valley.

"Up!" Huw shouted.

Arthur leapt to his feet, nearly tripping over them.

They ran from the forest, howling.

~ ~ ~

The startled Saxons recovered quickly, forming a circular clump, shields raised against the Cymry. Bedwyr locked eyes with a Saxon facing him and charged harder. Cai ran beside him, sword and shield swinging with each pounding step in time with his own. The eyes Bedwyr watched widened, the whites growing in the grubby face, and the invader's blade rose…then faltered as he took a half step backward. Bedwyr collided with him, and the Saxon fell. A slip of a shield, a glimpse of unprotected wool, and Bedwyr drove his blade down, through fabric and flesh, into the earth.

Jerking his sword free, he turned to the raider Cai had engaged. Two weapons against one, and soon that one too was down and gasping blood, and on to the next. They fell into a rhythm together, and then Bedwyr lost himself in the pulse of the fight. All movement around him slowed, giving him what felt like three seconds for every one. Opponents fell as if made of straw and wind, their mouths open on cries muted by the low-pressing sky. His sword became part of his body, his shield a wall no man could breach. Blood and steel fused in his spine, igniting fire down his limbs and out of his mouth, searing any Saxon fool enough to approach. He was a dragon of Cymru, son of his father's house and defender of this soil, these mountains—

A flash of copper sidewise. More fire, another dragon?

No, Arthur.

Bedwyr shook his head to clear it. Arthur was trying to face off against an invader twice as broad. Huw had planted himself half a pace in front of the lad, shielding him from the Saxon's blows. But Arthur, damn him, wasn't accepting the shield. Wasn't taking the opportunity to cut at the invader's ankles. Worse, he wasn't shielding Huw in turn. Instead, he was trying to strike the Saxon by reaching around Huw's shield. Then by stepping around it.

Idiot cub, he'd get himself killed.

"Bed!"

Ignoring Cai's surprised shout, Bedwyr weaved through the fight until he reached Arthur. With a rough shoulder, he shoved the lad back. "Stay behind!"

Arthur glared at him. "What?"

Bedwyr turned to the Saxon. Facing two Cymry now, the man showed his teeth and hacked at their shields. They would have been three against one, but Cai was somewhere behind Bedwyr, arguing with his brother. Bedwyr hadn't fought alongside Huw since his first skirmish, not enough to have a sense of the man's approach. He backed off, acting as an extra shield, eyes on the Saxon, his ears open to the scuffle behind him. Even above the shouting melee, he could make out Arthur's voice, angry, outraged, and aimed at the wrong opponent.

"I'll fight!"

And Cai's: "Stand down!"

The Saxon swiped viciously at Huw's knees. Bedwyr met the blow with his shield, and the impact drove him sideways. Regaining his stance, he delivered a strike to the Saxon that just missed his shoulder. The man turned crazed eyes on him.

Crazed meant unfocused. Bedwyr felt his strength surge. He was master of his body and his mind. Let them come, all the flailing, drooling Saxons who cared to slink up from their swamps. He had an answer to every one of their flinching, cowering jabs. Like maids sewing aprons they were, poking at him with their little bone needles. This one had a larger needle, he'd admit that, but it had no authority behind it. This Saxon's gods had abandoned him for their great casks of lowlander swill. He struck several blows, confounding the raider to the point of sputtering madness, before Huw stepped in to take the brunt once more.

Bedwyr drew a breath and raised his shield, preparing to deal a slice to the invader's legs, when that red hair streaked into his peripheral vision again. Instinctively, he threw his sword arm to the side to push Arthur back.

The cub threw him off. "What are you—?"

And then a tree hit Bedwyr's arm.

He stumbled, confused. The nearest trees…they were several yards away. Up the hill, and none were so tall. How could one have fallen on him? Was it a Saxon trick? He'd felt the weight of the thing. He looked around but…no trunk, no branch, not even a twig on the mud-slick ground.

Nothing but his sword. It lay in the snow, his glove still wrapped around the grip.

He'd lost his sword before but never his glove. He raised his hand to confirm it…

…but it wasn't there. His arm ended at the wrist.

The world tilted, and his knees hit the ground. He stared at where his hand should be, where instead blood pooled outward, licking ice-grains into itself.

Cai shouted. Arthur shouted. The Saxon shouted.

Everyone was shouting.

Bending forward, he set his forehead to the earth. It felt cool, smelled damp and calm. He breathed it in, his arm throbbing under him. His father's voice; it was always near him. Where was it now?

His shield settled over his head, and the world faded to dark silence.

CHAPTER 3

The next few minutes were chaos, and Arthur its beating heart.

Ignoring Cai, he charged the Saxon, knocking him flat on his back. The raider cried out and tried to bring both sword and shield to defend himself, but Arthur's ungainly landing splayed the man's arms. Without thought, he dragged his blade across the Saxon's throat, sending up a hot spray that blinded him temporarily. Staggering to his feet, he swiped at his eyes with a sleeve.

Huw had shifted to face another marauder. Bedwyr was gone. Arthur spun, looking for his body, then saw Cai dragging him away by the vest.

Bedwyr's sword still lay nearby.

Bedwyr's full glove gripped it.

Arthur swayed and looked away. *Focus. Saxons. How many?*

The boot-scuffed snow around him was littered with bodies. Men still fought, but the Cymry made up most of them. He was trying to decide which confrontation to join when a hand landed hard on his shoulder. He yelped.

Cai jerked him back and pointed to where Bedwyr lay near the tree line. "Go shield him!" he barked before shoving Arthur out of his way.

Arthur watched him go but couldn't move. Obey him or join him? Defend Bedwyr or kill more Saxons? There was Lord Uthyr, across the clearing, driving a raider back with his axe and sword. What would Uthyr have told him to do? Help the many or the one? The many, he would've said—never leave the fight.

But the one...

Bending, he scooped up Bedwyr's sword and ran toward the trees.

He lay where Cai had left him, sprawled beneath his shield. Arthur dropped Bedwyr's weapon—and gods, the glove, it still held on—and knelt beside the man. His face looked pale and slack, nothing like the expression Bedwyr usually wore, the quiet, neutral one that still managed somehow to be stern and intimidating.

He seemed neither now, only vulnerable in a way that made Arthur want to cover him with his own body. He rose to a crouch, weapon raised, but no one had ventured near. All the remaining men were either engaged in a clash or moaning in the snow.

Dropping his own armor, he knocked Bedwyr's shield aside. His injured arm lay against his belly, where blood had formed a dark, wet stain on the tanned hide of his winter vest.

Once, when he was a boy, Arthur had argued with Cai at the table and managed to slice his own palm deeply on Cai's eating knife. Their father had taken hold of Arthur's hand and lifted it above his head. "Hold it high for him," he'd told Cai. "Tightly at the wrist."

Arthur grabbed Bedwyr's arm and, finding where it ended under his sleeve, clamped his fingers around the wrist and held it above Bedwyr's unconscious form.

He shuddered. This was his doing. His fault. Bedwyr had lost his sword hand because Arthur had forgotten his training.

No. Not forgotten. *Discarded*, as if all the knowledge passed down to him had been useless in the face of his ambition.

He gripped Bedwyr's arm so tightly it shook.

Sometime later, Lord Uthyr appeared in front of him and pried his fingers from Bedwyr's arm. Tearing a leather cord from around his own neck, Uthyr wrenched it into a knot near Bedwyr's wrist. Then he uncurled the fingers of the glove from the sword grip and tossed the hand into Arthur's lap.

"Bury that."

Cradling it, Arthur rose and stumbled into the forest. Once inside the trees, he knelt in the snow and clawed at it until he'd made a hole in the loam of the forest floor. For one mad moment, he tried to decide if he should salvage the glove. But the thought of seeing the hand itself was enough to make him drop it into the hole. Bedwyr wouldn't be able to use the glove anyway, he told himself, scrabbling to cover everything over.

When he'd finished, he stared at the scarred ground for a long, churning moment before tipping sideways to vomit.

~ ~ ~

When Bedwyr came to next, steel-gray clouds scudded before him.

He lay on his back but not on the ground…he was bouncing too much for that. His head lolled as he tried to understand why the world looked as if it were upside-down, why trees passed him on both sides, why his right wrist felt as if it were clamped in a vise—

"He's awake!"

—why Cai sounded panicked. Cai didn't panic; he just got angry.

Then his father was there, between Bedwyr and the sky, and hadn't that always been the way of things? It calmed him.

"Can you hear me?"

"Yes." His voice sounded strange in his ears.

His father's face was grim under a spatter of mud and gore. "We're headed home."

Bedwyr tried to look around again. "The Saxons." Were the Cymry fleeing them?

"Dead," Uthyr said.

"Oh."

Then images began to spring up in his mind: a man's bared teeth…red hair…his sword…his glove—

His gorge rose. "Down," he choked. "Set me down!"

The earth hit him in the back. It made his teeth clack together and set his arm on fire. He rolled to one side and retched until nothing more would come. Dizzy and coughing, he slumped back onto the stretcher.

Cai stood at his feet, frowning. Arthur stood near him, his eyes wide and wary.

Uthyr's eyes held no such hesitance as he scanned the other men standing around them. "Two of you, relieve Huw and Cai. We're nearly halfway."

Two other faces leaned toward him, and then he was being lifted again.

The sky flowed past. The trees swam in its current.

His stomach floated, uncertain.

He swallowed the dregs of his nausea and passed out.

~

It was night when he woke again. The undersides of evergreen branches flickered overhead by the light of a fire, but the world didn't move otherwise. He exhaled in relief.

Then Master Matthias was there.

"Hello, Bedwyr."

The man's voice was as gentle as ever.

Bedwyr stared. Was he dreaming? Was he—

"Am I dead?"

Master Matthias smiled. "You are not, despite your best attempts."

The healer knelt beside him. At the hollow of his throat an iron nail hung from a leather thong. The man's father, old Marcus Roman, had worn the same. Bedwyr focused on it now. "How are you here?"

"Gwilym ran to fetch me. I daresay I slowed him down considerably on the way back."

"How long... Where are we?"

"You're about halfway home from where you were." Master Matthias pressed two fingers under Bedwyr's jaw. "Do you remember what happened, son?"

"My hand."

Matthias nodded.

"Am I going to die?"

"No," the healer scoffed quietly. "The gods wouldn't know what to do with you. You don't brag enough."

"Be straight with me."

The man set a cool palm to his forehead. "I'm going to make your life miserable for a few weeks. But you're strong. You'll survive it."

Did he want that? The Saxon had taken his sword hand. He could no longer fight. What good was a man of twenty-two who couldn't fight?

"Take this, lad."

Master Matthias lifted him from behind his shoulders. The man had the kind of wiry strength that other men often underestimated. Even Uthyr discounted it, despite the fact that Matthias was married to the single most intimidating woman in the village. The man was strong in ways others couldn't see. Bedwyr had always admired him for it.

He tried to smell what was in the cup.

"Go on. It will dull the pain so you can sleep. As soon as it's light tomorrow, I'll have to seal your wrist."

Bedwyr groaned.

Master Matthias squeezed his shoulder. "I know," he said in a low voice. He helped Bedwyr drink the brew down. It tasted bitter, like pond water tannic with walnut shells. "I'll be traveling with you and will mix this whenever you need it, all right?" He eased Bedwyr onto his back again.

"Thank you."

"Mix what?" Uthyr sounded like one of the carpenters' rasps compared to Cai's father. Bedwyr thought he saw Matthias school his expression, but it could have been a trick of the firelight.

"A remedy for the pain."

Uthyr gave the healer a disgusted look. Bedwyr glanced away before that expression could land on him.

"He needs to sleep if he's to bear the morning. Then to mend."

"To mend," Uthyr muttered. "What, he's going to grow another hand?"

"Uthyr." Master Matthias's voice was still low but its tone different now. More like years before, when he would give Cai a quiet warning.

"What, healer?"

Matthias stood, blocking Uthyr's face from Bedwyr's view. "You aren't helping."

"Helping?"

"You sent Gwilym to fetch me."

"A mistake."

"Mistake?"

Uthyr's hand swiped to the side in a dismissive gesture. "He's finished."

Frost seemed to form around Bedwyr's lungs.

"He can't fight. And if he can't fight, he can't lead. He's—"

"*Uthyr.*"

His father's boots crunched softly, planting themselves in the snow. Master Matthias said something too low for Bedwyr to hear. Uthyr's hand formed a fist, and Bedwyr thought perhaps he should warn the healer, but after a few seconds, Uthyr turned and stalked off. Matthias watched him go. Then he shifted as if he would look back at Bedwyr.

He shut his eyes against whatever the man's face might betray, and lay very still, his mind too noisy with his father's words to sense whether the remedy was working. A shuffle sounded near his elbow as Matthias retrieved the cup. Bedwyr waited for him to speak, hoped for it.

"He didn't mean it, Bedwyr."

Then wished he hadn't.

Matthias had never lied to him before.

~

For the first time since he'd begun to train as a warrior, Bedwyr opened his eyes on a dawn without his father's help.

The needled branches overhead ruffled in a breeze. Above the trees, the sky looked like unpolished steel. Blankets lay heavy atop him, heavier than usual. When he made to push them off, his right arm flashed with pain.

He grunted in surprise, and then with dread. His arm was pinned. Lifting the blankets with his left hand, he found his injured arm bound to his chest by a broad strip of cloth. He couldn't remember Master Matthias winding it about his ribs or tying it off.

Rolling his head, he looked about the camp. It lay quieter than usual, as if the men had gone. As if he'd been left—

He jerked upright, then gasped at the throbbing pain that brought.

"Easy." Quick footsteps brought Master Matthias. The healer knelt next to him and pressed on his shoulder. "Lie back."

He resisted, twisting to scan the camp. "Where is everyone?"

"Most have headed back. Your father sent them home." When Bedwyr met his eye, Matthias said, "We have work to do here."

His arm. Bedwyr's stomach churned. "What will you do?"

"Trim any ragged flesh. Cauterize it. Stitch you closed." The healer spoke matter-of-factly, as if he did these things every day. "Simple procedures," he said, as if he'd heard Bedwyr's thoughts. "But painful. I have something to dull it for you."

His father's words rang in his mind. "No."

"No remedy?"

"No remedy."

Matthias's brow creased in concern. "I strongly recommend you take it."

His father thought he was finished, but he was still master of himself. "No."

"Bedwyr—"

"Get it over with."

Matthias sighed. "Very well. I'll fetch the others."

"Others?"

"Uthyr kept a few men back."

"Why?"

"To hold you down."

Bedwyr's heart beat hard in his chest.

Matthias looked down the path, then leaned closer. "Will you take the remedy?"

And lose what little control he had left, with witnesses? "No."

"Stubborn," the healer muttered. "At least you come by it honestly."

He stepped away. The clink of coals behind Bedwyr's head spoke of a campfire he hadn't noticed. Matthias stirred them, then left to walk down the path.

Bedwyr would have known his father's boot steps anywhere. Uthyr stopped next to him, studying his face. "Are you clear-headed?"

"Yes."

His father looked at him for a long moment, his expression unreadable, then tipped his head. At the gesture, other men approached. Huw, Cai, Ifan, and Arthur.

Bedwyr glared at the cub. "Not him."

Arthur halted, glancing nervously at Bedwyr's father.

"He stays," Uthyr growled.

He directed Cai and his brother to each hold one of Bedwyr's legs. Ifan leaned hard on his good shoulder. Huw knelt next to his right one.

"I need you to keep his arm as still as possible," Matthias said to Huw, who nodded and locked it in a hard grip.

The first procedure hurt but no more than he could bear. *Trimming the flesh*, Matthias had called it, as ordinary and impersonal as dressing a deer. Bedwyr gritted his teeth and swallowed his voice at the slices of pain. One caught him out, and he shouted. A moment later, his father was pressing a stick against his teeth.

"Bite this."

"Don't need it."

Uthyr bent close. "You will soon. Open your jaw."

Reluctantly, he did so. His teeth sank into the bark. It tasted of resin.

After a few minutes, Matthias cleared his throat. "He's ready. Cai, Arthur—put your full weight into it. Huw…"

"Got it," Huw said.

"Uthyr?"

A scuffle sounded behind Bedwyr, and then his father's callused hand was pressing on his forehead. As best Bedwyr could tell, Uthyr had lain down, for then his voice grated in Bedwyr's ear.

"Courage."

The coals slid against each other again, and Bedwyr saw a brief flash of white-hot iron as Matthias stepped past Huw and knelt.

"Hold," Matthias said.

Weight bore down on his limbs, and then—

Fire!

He shouted as the blade seared him. Fire consumed his arm, his spine, his brain, and he bucked against it.

"Hold him!"

He fought them, the traitors pinning him to the ground, holding him to this fire that didn't come from within him as it should have done. A sound reached him, a sizzling, as of a rabbit on a spit, but he was too slow to shut his nose to it, and then he smelled his own flesh. He choked.

Matthias rose. "One down. Two more."

The coals released another blade, and Bedwyr shook his head. "Nuh…" The stick scraped his tongue.

His father's hand clamped tight. "The gods are watching," he hissed. "Be strong."

When Matthias reappeared, Bedwyr tried to pull his arm from Huw's grip, but the warrior held. The blade burned hotter this time, obliterating the sky. The stick fell from his mouth, was jammed back in.

"One more," his father said.

Bedwyr made a sound he wished he could take back. Then made it more loudly when the third blade melted into him.

The burn kept on even after Matthias tossed the dagger aside. Bedwyr writhed against it, wanting nothing more than to shove his arm into the surrounding snow.

"Almost finished," Matthias said. "Keep him still, please."

He didn't feel the stitches. The maids' bone needles were real now, only he was the apron they hemmed. He lay limp, staring at the pine branches.

They should have done it, these men. They should have left him here.

Sometime later, Matthias sat back. "That's that."

Slowly, the pressure eased from his limbs as the men released him. He closed his eyes, unable to meet theirs. One by one, they stepped away. The hard heat of his father's hand left his forehead, and the chill of the morning made him shiver. He waited for the words, the ones that would tell him if he'd borne this like a warrior.

They didn't come. Only a creak of leather as Uthyr rose and walked away.

When Bedwyr opened his eyes, the pines were still. Matthias knelt next to him. He set a cool hand to the side of Bedwyr's face and gave him a weary smile.

"I'm proud of you."

The evergreen branches overhead wavered, and then he couldn't hold it in. He turned his face into Matthias's knee and wept as quietly as he could.

CHAPTER 4

At home, Bedwyr slept, grateful for the healer's potions.

A few people came and went from his bedside. His sister, Gwen, with hot broth and a worried expression. Cai less frequently, with hands so fidgety Bedwyr began to pretend sleepiness to shorten his visits. Once, the rugs hanging around his bed parted, and Arthur stepped through them.

The urge to crawl backward into his bedding gripped him hard. "What do you want?"

The cub's steps stuttered. "I…" Then he only stood there, fists clenching. Both of them.

Bedwyr glared at him. "Go away."

"I'm sorry, Bedwyr. I don't—"

"Get out!"

When Arthur swallowed whatever he might have said next and left, upright and whole, Bedwyr slammed his arm against the bedding in frustration. He writhed in pain, swearing through gritted teeth.

Footsteps crossed the space toward him.

"I said *leave*."

"And I'm going to claim to know better."

He opened his eyes to Master Matthias. Bedwyr fought to regain control of his breath. "Sorry. I thought…"

"Yes, I heard."

He lay still as Matthias set his wooden case on the bench next to the bed. With his usual care, he pulled a clay jar from the case. How had someone as reckless as Arthur come from a man so measured?

Sitting on the edge of the mattress, Matthias helped him up and held the jar while he drank the flatly bitter remedy. When he lay back again, Matthias set aside the jar.

"All right, let's see you."

He lifted Bedwyr's injured arm onto his belly. Cradling his elbow in one large hand, he unwrapped the stump. When he prodded at the angry seam, Bedwyr couldn't feel it. The pain was deeper, somewhere in the bone, maybe. The medicine began to seep into his consciousness, softening the sharp sensations, but he didn't want the healer to leave yet.

"It hurts farther up."

Matthias glanced at his face, studying his eyes, then his fingers moved up Bedwyr's arm. He pressed with his thumb. "Here?"

Not there—not really—but the healer's hands grounded him. "On the inside."

Matthias shifted his hold and massaged gentle circles on the underside of Bedwyr's forearm.

He was wrong to use the man like this, to detain him just for the touch. To take advantage of his nature, which had always shown compassion when others hadn't.

But he needed it. Keenly.

"You wear a nail," he said.

"I do."

"So did Master Marcus."

"And you bear dragons in ink, like your father."

He didn't want to think about his father. "Why?"

"Why?"

"Why a nail?"

Matthias's warm hands shifted toward his elbow. "Marcus's foster father made one for him just before he left home to join the army. It was how Papa recognized him when he returned. When I was a boy, he forged this one to match it."

"Mass-ter Wolf?" He seemed to trip on the words. The remedy would claim him soon.

"Yes."

Bedwyr reached for the nail. His hand was unsteady and bumped Matthias's chest before his fingers found the iron. "'S it remind you of 'em?"

Matthias smiled. "It does. Papa very neatly created something that would keep both my fathers close to my heart."

Bedwyr flattened his hand and pressed it to Matthias's breastbone. He felt two thumps of the man's heart before Matthias covered his hand with his own and drew it away.

"Time to rest, son."

"Don't go."

He sounded pathetic, but Matthias only squeezed his hand. "I'll stay for the moment. Let the remedy take you, Bedwyr."

That didn't make sense. Remedies didn't take people; it went the other way 'round. He opened his mouth to tell Matthias so, but the room was taking on a strange rippling quality, as if it had filled with water. Bedwyr closed his mouth. Held his breath.

Sank into the deep.

~

Three weeks later, as the winter sun sank early toward sleep, Matthias removed the stitches he had used to close Bedwyr's arm. It looked gnarled, this wrist that was no longer a wrist. His skin no longer bore the angry redness of before. Matthias had made neat work of it, considering. Bedwyr probably should have felt more thankful. Instead, he was on a blade's edge.

They sat at the table, Matthias straddling the bench before him, his head bent to his work. Gwen hovered at the hearth, pretending to be busy. Uthyr paced nearby. Bedwyr bit down against the pull of the thread and tried to ignore the unrest in the chamber, to draw calm from the healer's hands.

Uthyr dismissed the man as soon as he finished. Matthias gave Bedwyr a look that was probably meant to encourage, but he only nodded back. His father had something on his mind. The sooner he spoke, the better.

He didn't waste any time. "What happened?"

Panic licked at Bedwyr's belly. Had Uthyr heard the way he'd spoken to Matthias under the remedies? Seen his clumsy pawing?

But then Uthyr said, "During the skirmish."

The skirmish. Of course. He insisted on reports from his men, and his son was no different in that regard. "I was distracted."

"By Arthur?"

The sudden accuracy pulled him up short.

Uthyr was staring hard at him. "Cai said his brother was out of formation, ignoring his responsibility to Huw. Huw confirmed it."

That look in his father's eyes. He would pass judgment, as was his right, but...

His verdict would be final, and Arthur had only eighteen years under his belt.

"No, it was another Saxon. I let myself lose focus."

"Another Saxon." Not a question. Not a statement with any belief behind it, either. "Are you protecting the boy?"

"No."

"He cost you your sword hand."

"He didn't. I was careless—"

"Enough."

He sat, pulse pounding as Uthyr began to pace again. Gwen had stopped fiddling with the fire and was watching their father, her face drawn. Bedwyr's arm throbbed. He pressed it to his belly.

Uthyr stalked back to him. "Go to the shepherd's hut."

Bedwyr stared at him, trying to make sense of the words.

"The one to the northeast is empty. Go there."

"Why, Ta?" Gwen said.

But Bedwyr knew why. There was no reason for him to remain here. He couldn't fight. He couldn't follow his father in battle or lead men. He was finished, and Uthyr was finished with him.

"I'm for the armory," Uthyr rumbled. "You'll be gone before I return."

Gwen reached for him. "Ta, no!"

Uthyr gave her a firm look. "I've spoken, Gwenhwyfar."

His sister pulled back, uncharacteristically abashed.

Uthyr left the house, and all sensation of anything real left with him.

Bedwyr rose, leaned against the table for a moment, then turned for his bed and the pegs that held his clothes. Numbly, he began to stuff them into a sack, grunting in frustration when he couldn't hold it open.

A hand on his arm stilled him. With quiet, jerky movements, Gwen took over. She seemed bent on packing everything, though, so he lifted the bag away from her.

"Your cloak."

"Gwen—"

"Wait."

She fetched it from the hook by the door and draped it over his shoulders. When she stepped around to clasp it at his throat, he ground his teeth. "I'm not a child."

She avoided his eyes. When she'd finished, she hugged him around the neck. "I'll come up tomorrow," she said softly in his ear.

He couldn't muster a response, not for Gwen nor for the few others he passed on his way out of the village. The last person he saw was Mistress Britte at her anvil at the edge of the settlement. Everything in the smithy glowed with a foreign warmth—fire pan, lantern, even the smith's hair, the same color as her cub's. Bedwyr turned away from it.

The hike to the hut took only a quarter of an hour but its location beyond a broad hill made it seem as if he'd crossed into another lord's lands. Might as well have done. With no shepherd lads or sheep to clear the snow on the path, he had to trudge through it. No one had come this way in some time, and no one would soon. As the sky dimmed toward night, he wondered if the hut was only a way station—if, come the spring thaw, Uthyr would send him on over the mountains. One boot slipped and he fought for balance through a cloud of his own breath. It cooled on his skin, sending a chill down his back.

The small hut sat empty, its thatch dark against the deep slate sky. When he shouldered the door open, it fell off its hinges onto the packed-dirt floor. Too weary to face the prospect of repairing it one-handed, or even of building a fire, he threw his pack into a corner. The musty bunk creaked under him as he lay down and rolled toward the wall.

He didn't sleep.

~ ~ ~

The great chair sat empty again. Three nights and counting.

Arthur had never seen it like this. Lord Uthyr had been absent before, certainly, but because of patrols or campaigns. Never when the lord was in the village. Illness didn't seem to affect him; even when Arthur's father had had to treat Uthyr for something, the lord always took up his place at the evening fire. Arthur hadn't realized how much his warlord's presence grounded him until the man wasn't there.

The village had been shocked by Bedwyr's injury. What should have been a victory celebration upon the warriors' return had been a subdued gathering. No man sought new ink. People gathered in small, somber groups unwilling to voice their uncertainty but unable to keep the questions from their eyes. How had such a thing befallen the son of the Pen y Ddraig. A warrior so skilled? A young man so level-headed? Their heir?

Between Cai and Huw, everyone learned of Arthur's role in the disaster. From where he sat with his back pressed to one wall, he watched his brother go from huddle to huddle, bore their gazes when they stared at him. No one shunned him outright, but they began to avoid him, as if even a word with him might injure them as well. His cheeks felt hot with shame day and night, but he couldn't let himself escape the weight of his neighbors' judgment. To do so would be cowardly. He had to show himself, to make it right somehow.

He'd tried, once. A week after their return, he'd accompanied his father to see Bedwyr. While his father took a seat at the table and began to talk quietly with Gwen, Arthur approached the hangings that designated Bedwyr's sleeping area. He'd thought and thought over what he should say, but the closer he got to the rugs, the more the words jumbled in his mind. When he stepped through them, the sight of Bedwyr's pale, listless form gave him pause. He'd begun stumbling through an apology, but Bedwyr had surged up and shouted him out. He hadn't been able to look at his father or Gwen as he fled the house.

He hadn't tried again, despite his father's urging. Forget his stupid fantasies of the warlord's son. He'd forfeited even the chance to serve him as a friend. Bedwyr would never want to see his face again.

Then, three evenings ago, whispers had passed about the hall that Lord Uthyr had sent Bedwyr away. When Mora told Arthur, he'd felt sick. Only one other person had been banished in his memory. That man had made the mistake of trying to seduce Uthyr's woman. Arthur had stolen his heir, whereas Bedwyr had only tried to protect him. If Bedwyr had been banished for that, what would his own punishment be?

He'd been waiting to find out. He might have gathered the courage to speak to Lord Uthyr, but Huw had put it about that the man wanted no company. He spent his days and nights in the armory, and short of a Saxon horde's arrival, no one was to disturb him.

And so Arthur had avoided the armory, knowing full well he didn't have the courage to do otherwise. In the hall, he pressed back into the wall, hearing only bits of Tiro's tales, and staring at his two useless hands.

There he was this night, when someone came to sit next to him. Glancing up, surprised, he found Master Philip there.

"How are you, Arthur?"

He looked back to his hands. "How do you suppose?"

Master Philip was quiet long enough that Arthur wished him away. But his old teacher wasn't so easily put off. "Do you remember our lessons about justice?"

Arthur's fists clenched involuntarily.

"What are the conditions of justice?" Philip asked softly.

"The wronged party determines justice," he said, the response almost automatic.

"And?"

"No man may be asked to repay more than he can give."

"That's correct." Master Philip was quiet again, and Arthur wondered what sort of torture this was, as Philip then spent a long moment watching Tiro tell his tale. But then he said, "I've had a good, long life so far to reflect on justice. I would add one more condition."

Arthur swallowed the sour taste in his mouth. "What's that?"

Philip considered him. His eyes seemed unexpectedly kind. "When possible, we must craft a form of rehabilitation that suits the particular injustice."

Arthur rolled those words around in his head, but before he could make much sense of them, Philip spoke again.

"Lord Uthyr wishes to see you."

~

A slash of light shone under the armory door. Not allowing his steps to slow, Arthur pushed open the door and stepped inside. Two lamps burned on the wall above one of the workbenches. Lord Uthyr stood there, surrounded by weapons, and it occurred to Arthur he might be about to die, and rightfully so.

"My lord."

Uthyr gave him a long, hard stare. When he spoke, it was quietly, but Arthur didn't miss a word.

"I'll keep this brief. I don't know why Bedwyr felt the need to come between you and that Saxon dog. But if you had fought in the manner you were trained, he would still be whole. You cost my son his sword hand. And so I've been thinking about what your cost should be."

Arthur began to shake.

Your cost.

It could be only one thing.

Stepping up to the workbench, he pushed up his sleeve and set his sword hand on the wooden table. He spread his fingers, pressing their tips into the grain, memorizing the feel of it.

He waited.

A very long moment later, Uthyr said, "Put that away."

Arthur jerked his hand from the table. Sucking a breath he sorely needed, he curled his fingers tightly into the safety of his palm. When he looked at Uthyr, the man's eyes were still impenetrable.

"He's at the shepherd's hut to the northeast," Uthyr said. "You're going to take your gear and his, and go there. You're going to see that he learns how to handle his sword with his left hand. You're not going to tell him I sent you."

He looked at Uthyr's massive shoulders, his square skull. Bedwyr was built of the same immovable stuff.

"You look as though you need more incentive," Uthyr said. "Here it is: you retrain my son, or neither of you is welcome to return."

The armory tilted slightly. He fought the visceral urge to grab the workbench to steady himself.

"Do you understand me, Arthur ap Matthias?"

"Yes, my lord."

Uthyr handed him a sword and shield that had lain on the workbench—Bedwyr's armor. "Go."

CHAPTER 5

"It was my fault. I want to help him."

Arthur's parents, seated on the other side of the table, gave each other a long, silent look.

The household had been strained for weeks, what with Cai not speaking to him. Mora had gone too far in the opposite direction, chattering nervously until their mother threatened to muzzle her. Their father had tried to ease the tension, but some things weren't in a healer's power to mend.

When his parents turned back to him now, his father's eyes held concern but he didn't refute Arthur's guilt. His hands shuffled restlessly on the tabletop, as if he wanted to offer comfort.

Arthur kept his own on his thighs. He wouldn't tell them about the order Lord Uthyr had just given him, imagining a humiliating scenario in which they appealed to the warlord on his behalf. He was a man and would act like one.

"His shield will need to be refitted," his mother said.

Arthur let out a breath. He'd known she would understand.

At dawn the next morning, he followed her the short distance to the smithy, just across the main path from their family's house. As his mother lit a lantern, he looked about the place, unable to accept he might not see it again. He'd grown up under its roof and single rear wall, where the hand tools hung from their pegs. Two great log sections held the larger anvils, which flanked the fire pan served by the forge. Though his mother had an apprentice and had run the workshop for most of Arthur's life, the space still felt half empty.

That she rarely used the largest anvil, the one his grandfather had worked over, only made the sensation stronger.

Arthur watched while she fitted Bedwyr's thick oak shield with straps that would help keep it on his short arm, using Arthur as a mannequin as best she could. When she handed him the altered shield, she finally spoke. "Be good to that boy."

"He's a man, Mama."

"His age doesn't matter. He's been banished by his father." She looked about to say something else, and he could imagine the general color of the sentiment. His mother had a strange grudge against Lord Uthyr. But her next words surprised him. "Promise me you'll treat him well."

It was odd to hear such a thing from his mother. She didn't beg promises. "I'm going up there to help him."

She gripped him by the back of his neck. "He's lost more than his hand. You remember that."

This tone was closer to what he was accustomed to. "I will."

"Arthur."

"What?"

Her hand eased up then, and she gave the queue of his hair a light tug. "Just don't give up on him."

She looked at him for a long moment, and he had the urge to tell her everything—that he couldn't give up on Bedwyr or himself, that if he didn't succeed she wouldn't see him again—but the words only crowded the back of his tongue until she let him go and walked back to their family's house without him.

~

He was deep in his thoughts, trying to decide what he should say first, when Gwen caught up to him on the path.

"Where are you headed?"

He eyed the cloth-draped basket in the crook of her arm. "Same place you are." He hitched the heavy campaign pack on his back, and the armor in it clanked.

She eyed it shrewdly. "Planning to make a nuisance of yourself?"

"An extended one."

"Arthur—"

"I have to."

He considered telling Gwen about her father's ultimatum. They'd been friends for a long time, and she probably would help him. This wasn't going to be easy, judging by the way Bedwyr had told him off when he tried to apologize a couple of weeks before. But the man had had every right to do so. This wasn't supposed to be easy.

Still, he wasn't too proud to admit to himself that he was glad for her company.

She stepped around him with a dubious look, and he fell in behind her on the path, watching her swinging plait to distract him from the task ahead.

He didn't remember her mother; he'd been a babe himself when she'd died bringing Gwen into the world. Everyone said she'd been a pale beauty, almost ghostly. Not frail, exactly, but not muscular like his own mother. There must have been some strength in her, Arthur figured, for Gwen looked just like her. Everyone said so. Her name even meant *fair*. Master Philip had taught him that dark hair usually won over light when it came to babes resembling their parents. That was plain enough to see with Bedwyr. But Gwen's hair looked like moonlight. Some in the village thought she'd had been touched by a fairy as a babe, for the only things she shared with her father were her dark eyes. As befitted a warlord's daughter, she wielded them like weapons.

It was a wonder he'd ever managed to keep anything from her.

What would she say if she knew what sort of thoughts he'd had about her brother and dark corners?

"Is he well?" he asked.

She shrugged. "He eats."

"But is he *well*?"

She glanced at him over her shoulder. "Well?"

"You know...himself."

"He lost his sword hand. No, he isn't himself."

She didn't say it accusingly, only with admonition. She'd treated him well, considering what he'd done. Besides hurting her brother, he might have harmed Gwen's future too if Bedwyr couldn't succeed his father—she would have no blood tie to the next warlord. Arthur let that prospect fire his determination to get Bedwyr fighting again.

"When I showed up yesterday," Gwen said, "he was lying down. He got up to eat, but only when I threatened to spoon it into his mouth like a babe." She looked at Arthur and seemed about to say something, then shook her head, frowning.

"What?"

She stopped and turned to him. "The door of the hut has come off its hinges. I offered to send Dafydd up to fix it, but he got angry, told me not to do it. He hadn't bothered to build a fire, either."

Arthur looked at the snow-drifted curve of path ahead.

"Don't get your hopes up," Gwen said, her eyebrows pinched together. "He doesn't want to see anyone. Said your father is the only person he could stand to have around."

"And you."

She shrugged. "He tolerates me."

He nudged her with an elbow. "What's your secret?" he asked, only half teasing.

She lifted the basket with a rueful smile.

"Does your father know you bring him food?"

Her chin rose. "He couldn't stop me."

There was the Gwen he knew.

The little hut stood on the far side of a hill, surrounded by land that, in spring and summer, provided grazing for sheep and goats. Snow blanketed everything now, a hand-span deep. As they approached, he looked for signs that anyone occupied the hut, but didn't see any. No smoke rose from the stubby chimney, and the door leaned against its frame as if left there for the past five winters. The whole thing seemed empty. He squeezed his hands, then flexed them, trying to shake off his nerves. It wasn't as if he were heading into battle, was it?

As they neared the building, Gwen began to whistle. He recognized the tune from when they had scampered about as brats. He was trying to remember the words when the door of the hut shifted to the side.

Bedwyr stood under the lintel, his injured arm shielded by the door. When he caught sight of Arthur, he straightened. His face was pale, with smudges under his eyes that made them look darker. He leveled a flat look at Gwen. "Why did you bring him here?"

"He—"

"I followed her," Arthur said.

"There's nothing here for you." Bedwyr let Gwen pass under his arm. "Go home, cub."

Before Arthur could respond, Bedwyr set the door back into

place, shutting him out.

It was no more or less than he had expected, but he wasn't going home.

He set his pack against the side of the hut. Clearing the ground under the eaves of snow, he laid out his bedroll, then sat down and dug through his pack for the bread and cheese he'd raided from his mother's cellar. He gnawed through the flavors of his boyhood—sourdough and sharp, grassy sheep's milk—then set about gathering firewood.

Gwen left half an hour later with an apologetic wave.

Bedwyr emerged once, glaring first at Arthur's bedroll, then at him, before tromping to the far side of the hut, presumably to piss. When he returned, he avoided Arthur's gaze and shoved the door to.

Day wore on, and night fell. No light shone from inside the hut—no fire, no lantern. The wind buffeting the hill carried the scent of new snow. The flakes began to fall an hour later.

Burrowing into his blankets, he huddled against the hut, taking what shelter from it he could.

~

The following day, Arthur intercepted Gwen on the path. This time, he wrangled for the basket. After a minor struggle, she gave it up to him.

"What do you think you'll accomplish?"

"I don't know."

"I don't either."

But she let him walk away, the heavy basket swinging from one hand.

When he neared the hut, he began to whistle the same tune Gwen had. The door opened, and Bedwyr stood just inside, his brows knit.

"Where's Gwen?"

"In the village."

"What do you want?"

"To give you this." He handed the basket to the other man.

Bedwyr took it.

"May I come in?"

"No."

"Do you need a fire built—"

"No."

"I can—"

Bedwyr stepped back and shut the door.

~

Gwen approached Arthur with a resigned expression on the third day. She looked at him for a long moment, then nodded at the basket. "I put extra oat bread in there."

He grinned.

He knew her well enough to see her try not to smile back. "Don't need you both starving," she muttered, squinting back toward the village.

"Thanks, Gwen."

She waved him off with a scowl. "Go on."

This time he gave Bedwyr no advance warning by whistle, but the man opened the door as soon as he came into view of the hut.

"My sister grows uglier every day."

"That's the hunger talking." He held up the basket. "Good thing I brought this."

Bedwyr took it, then frowned at Arthur's pack, which still rested against the hut. "Going on a journey?"

"Yes."

Dark eyes narrowed, wary. "With weapons?"

"Yes."

"To where?"

"To here."

Bedwyr stared at the pack, then Arthur. "You can't stay here."

"There's no bed?"

"There's no *second* bed."

Arthur shrugged. "I brought a bedroll," he said, waving to where it lay. "I'll sleep on the floor."

"You won't."

"No?"

"No!"

"Gwen packed extra bread—may I have some?"

"Fuck off!" Bedwyr mashed the door back into place, leaving him outside.

Arthur could have opened the door. He could have pushed it

aside, easily. If he'd wanted to, he could have extracted it from the hut and tossed it onto the hillside, leaving the small building with no barrier at all.

But Bedwyr had closed it. He wanted that barrier.

And it wasn't fair how easy it would have been for Arthur to remove it.

He left it in place and waited.

~

Three more days, as it turned out.

Each morning, he rose and gathered firewood for several hours, stacking it against the outer wall of the hut. Bedwyr glared at the pile every time he came out of the building, which seemed to be only to relieve himself. He didn't acknowledge Arthur except to pointedly ignore him. Someone—Gwen, Arthur supposed—had pinned Bedwyr's sleeve at his stump. He walked with it tucked into his ribs.

Gwen came each midday with her basket. Arthur didn't interfere anymore as she delivered the food. He did try to overhear what the siblings said to each other, but while he could make out Gwen's voice, her brother's was no louder or more intelligible than a distant rumble of thunder.

He was able to make that comparison on the third day, when a storm began to build to the west. Gwen frowned at the dark, rolling clouds as she left the hut.

"You're going to get wet," she said.

"Maybe."

She surveyed the hills, then lowered her voice. "Has anyone else come up?"

"No."

Glancing at the hut, she set her jaw. "I think he's in pain and won't admit it."

"Tell Papa."

"I did," she said. "He sent me with a remedy, but Bed won't take it."

"Where is it?"

"I left it on the table."

"He'll take it, just not in front of you."

"That's stupid."

He shrugged, to which she rolled her eyes.

"Stay dry."

Within the hour, icy rain swept over the mountains in thick gray swathes. He rolled up his bedding and tried to stand under the shelter afforded by the hut's thatching. It was too low for him, though, and he had to squat, which ensured that the chilly water running off the roof drenched his legs. As the storm pounded away, he felt more than heard the shift of the door. He almost couldn't make out Bedwyr's scowl.

Almost.

"Get inside," Bedwyr growled.

Arthur wasted no time, pushing past the man and into the relative dryness of the small hut's interior. Throwing his pack against one wall, he opened the door again.

"What—"

Bedwyr's voice was lost in the thrum of the sleet as Arthur rounded the hut to the stack of firewood. The material resting directly against the building was dry, and he filled his arms with as much as he could carry.

Bedwyr stared as he ducked back under the lintel. "What are you doing?"

"Building a fire."

"I don't want a fire."

"Too bad. I do."

"It'll be too hot."

"So strip."

The other man glared at him.

"Or don't." He knelt by the hearth and set down the fuel. "Gwen said she left a remedy for you."

"And?"

"You should take it."

"Don't need it."

"Don't need fire, don't need remedies." He looked at Bedwyr over his shoulder. "Anything else?" When Bedwyr glowered and opened his mouth, Arthur held up a hand. "On second thought, don't answer that."

Silence fell as he built the fire, broken only by the smack of ice pellets against the door. He got the fire going quickly, a feat since his hands shook with chill.

"Why are you here?"

It sounded as if Bedwyr had pushed the words through his teeth. Arthur stood, catching himself just short of knocking his skull on a rafter. He tried for humor. "You invited me in."

The humor found no welcome, only the same glare he'd seen for days. He was going to have to come clean. Just...not all the way. Crossing to his pack, he lifted the large flap to reveal the gear.

Bedwyr's black eyes flicked to it.

"One set's mine," Arthur said. "The other is yours."

Bedwyr's attention jerked back to him.

"You're going to learn how to use it again."

The man held up his stump. "And who's going to work that miracle?"

He would have liked to give a cocky response but couldn't. Some bit of truth was needed here. "You are."

When dark eyebrows rose in surprise, Arthur pressed his advantage.

"You're not scared, are you?"

Bedwyr's remaining fist clenched hard. He looked as if he was trying to decide if he could strangle Arthur one-handed.

He didn't. Nor did he drag him to the door and heave him out into the storm.

Acting as unaffected as he could, Arthur spread his bedroll before the hearth, then stripped off his cold, wet clothes and hung them over the rafters. By the time he slid under the blankets, his new hut mate had done the same.

The fire crackled, warm and dry.

It was a start.

CHAPTER 6

Bedwyr didn't wake up to a hand on his throat, but he might as well have done.

Instead, he woke to the sight of a bare, muscular back hunched before the hearth. A slip of the gaze gave him the long curve of Arthur's wool-clad thighs. Trying to escape that, he looked up sharply, just in time to see the flex of his biceps as he set a log on the grate.

Bedwyr groaned.

Arthur looked at him over one shoulder. "Want some bread?"

"Water," he said and immediately regretted admitting the need, as Arthur stood to fetch some. "I'll get it," Bedwyr grumped.

Arthur stopped in his tracks. "Suit yourself." He went back to building the fire.

Bedwyr had been awake all of twenty breaths, and he was already grinding his teeth.

"How's your arm?"

The question brought his attention to his stump. It began to throb. "Fine."

"Good. We can start today."

"Start what?"

"Don't play stupid."

As Bedwyr clamped his jaw on a retort, Arthur bent forward to blow on his fire.

Bedwyr sat up and grabbed his shirt. The packed-dirt floor was cold on his feet. At least he'd left his trousers on and wouldn't have to fumble with the laces in front of present company.

This day couldn't end soon enough.

He trudged to the small table on which he'd set Gwen's offerings each midday. Several oat bannocks lay in a cloth there, along with a crock of the goat's cheese she knew he liked. She hadn't realized yet that a man needed two hands to spread the soft cheese onto an oatcake, and he hadn't felt like pointing it out. Grumpy, he picked up a dry bannock and glared at it. They were better with cheese.

Without warning, Arthur appeared next to him. Grabbing the small paddle Gwen had left, Arthur scooped a generous dollop of cheese from the crock and mashed it across a bannock. Swiftly, he took the naked one from Bedwyr and replaced it with the loaded one. Before Bedwyr could protest a word, Arthur piled cheese on the dry oatcake and shoved it into his own mouth, already reaching for a third.

"Eaddup," he mumbled around the food.

"Fuck off," Bedwyr murmured back.

Arthur looked at him. "Fine thanks."

Bedwyr took a large bite, chewing it openmouthed in a way Gwen would have smacked him for.

The cub only nodded, then swallowed. He ate the third bannock, deftly slipping a fourth into Bedwyr's hand as soon as it was empty.

He briefly considered mashing it against the side of Arthur's face, but the cheese was too tasty, damn the stuff. As the other man turned away, Bedwyr savored its creamy tang. Gwen had stirred herbs into it, giving him an impression of summer even as his breath floated in the cold air before him.

"Hold out your arm."

Bedwyr raised his right arm on instinct. He began to lower it, sheepish, but Arthur nodded.

"That one."

He lifted Bedwyr's shield from the small pile of armor against the wall. He turned the inside toward Bedwyr, revealing a tangle of leather straps.

"What're those?"

Arthur glanced at him, only a brief flash of gray eyes before he worked loose one of the straps. "I asked my mother to fit something for you. So you could use your…right arm."

He could only imagine how futile Mistress Britte had considered that request. Even so, she'd done it. Maybe she had an irrational soft spot for her younger son.

Arthur teased some sort of sense of the harness, and he slipped a loop over Bedwyr's stump and up his arm. He worked the straps around his elbow and began to tighten them, tugging periodically to seat the shield. He smelled of the fire he'd built in the hearth. Bedwyr held his breath as Arthur's hard fingers made the adjustments. At least he was fairly confident. Anything less would have tried Bedwyr's patience.

"Where'd you get my gear?"

"I took it."

Bedwyr stared at him.

Arthur wouldn't meet his eyes. "Gwen helped."

"She gave it to you?" He'd have words for his sister next he saw her.

"No, she told me where to find it while Lord Uthyr was at the story fire."

An incredulous laugh escaped him.

Arthur looked up. "What?"

"You entered my father's house and stole my armor?"

"Yes."

That was all he had to say? "You're either brave or stupid."

Arthur's eyes shifted away again. "Not for me to say. Here." He handed Bedwyr his sword.

It was too heavy, out of balance. It felt strange, the grooves on the grip all wrong for his left hand, as if he held another man's cock. He flexed his fingers and dropped it.

Arthur retrieved it, handing it back without a word.

Bedwyr studied him as he gathered his own gear. Arthur ap Matthias didn't do anything silently. He always had something to say, often to his detriment. What was different now?

When they stepped outside, Bedwyr scanned the area, then felt foolish. Who would be spying on them? Still, he felt awkward enough not to want anyone to see it. He hitched the shield on his right arm, chafing at the new straps. Chafing at everything. But then Arthur turned and planted his feet, and forced him to do the same or look a coward.

He wasn't a coward. He needed very much to believe that just now. He gripped his sword hard.

"Relax your hand."

He obeyed before he realized he had done so or that Arthur had noted his tension. He rolled his shoulders to ease his discomfort. What else was the cub noticing?

Arthur cleared his throat. "Do you remember what my grandfather used to say about fighting someone opposite-handed?"

Don't, Master Marcus had said, *if you can avoid it.* It put fighters' weapons on the same side and limited their shields' effectiveness. If Arthur swung high or wide with his right arm, Bedwyr's shield—on his right arm—would have to cross his body to defend it.

On the other hand, so to speak, if a man was a strong fighter, he could deliberately seek opposite-handed opponents because they would have a more difficult time defending themselves.

He wasn't strong, not anymore. "It's difficult to defend."

"Right. So let's level the ground." With deft motions, Arthur switched his shield to his right hand, his sword to his left.

"You're joking."

"I'm not."

"What's the use if we're both weak-handed?"

"That's the point."

"We'll look like idiot—"

Arthur swung.

Bedwyr raised his shield on instinct to block the blow. It wasn't a hard one and glanced off his shield's rim. Still, his heart beat in his ears.

"Who cares what we look like?" Arthur said. "Who's watching but the gods?"

"Oh, piddling audience."

Arthur shrugged, his jaw set.

Fine. They'd do this and look like the fools they were. Maybe if he gave hard enough, the cub would tire of this game and go home. Leave him in peace. He gripped his sword and struck.

Arthur defended himself, not without ducking his head, and the goosey look of it was enough to fuel another strike. The lad didn't retreat more than a couple of steps, though, and soon he was holding his ground, delivering his own strikes. They traded blows for several minutes, Bedwyr unwilling to be the one who backed down first.

Eventually, Arthur stepped to the side. "Hold."

They stood there, breathing thick steam into the winter air. If the gods were watching…

Arthur moved to adjust his shield, his expression one of determination. Abashed, Bedwyr checked the seating of his own shield, tightened the straps Mistress Britte had put on it. Rolling the sword in his hand, he tried to find a grip that didn't feel so strange. It was his weapon, damn the thing.

"Ready?"

As he'd ever be. "Ready."

They sparred again, and again it was tiring and pointless. He couldn't control his sword well enough to choose deliberately between the edge and the flat of the blade. His hold on the shield was even more tenuous. When he resorted finally to hugging it to his body, it became useless, forcing him to throw himself at Arthur's blade just to deflect it.

They stepped apart, chests heaving. Arthur's face was red. His own must carry the same flush. He willed his heart to slow, and winced as he straightened his cramping right arm.

"No shields," Arthur said.

"What?"

"Swords only, this time." Arthur lifted his chin. "Fundamentals."

Fundamentals. "You sound like Marcus Roman."

Arthur tossed his shield to the side. It landed on the snow with a soft thud.

Bedwyr started to do the same then realized he needed to unfasten the harness.

Arthur stepped toward him.

"I've got it," Bedwyr muttered. Setting his sword against one leg, he yanked at the strips of leather until his arm was free. He flung the thing off him with more force than was probably necessary and picked up his sword.

He hadn't sparred without a shield in years. This took him straight back to his boyhood, when Master Marcus had made Cai and him face off with wooden practice swords. When they'd begged for shields, he'd told them they were too fucking clumsy to handle two things at once. He'd made them wait three full years for shields, and only gave them over after the boys swore their free hands weren't busy jerking their pricks.

As he renewed his grip on his blade, Bedwyr studied Arthur. He was taller than Master Marcus had ever been, and almost fifty years younger than the old Roman soldier when he'd begun to train Bedwyr and Cai.

But growing up as Marcus's grandson had had its effect. Arthur was a good fighter. He practiced, certainly, but Marcus's daily influence on his mind and awareness had shaped him in a way Bedwyr envied. The younger man seemed to understand certain things instinctively. He was brash, to be sure, but just now, with no enemy threatening to strike him down and no commander to impress, he had his head on straight. His stance was calm and confident. He inhabited his body, utterly.

It made Bedwyr's cock twitch, and he had no idea what to do with that.

So he fought. It was odd to have no shield. Made him feel exposed, and he was over-aware of how his short arm flailed to keep his balance.

But it freed him too. All he had to concentrate on was his sword arm—his grip, his swing, his parry. As the clouds scudded overhead, the men sparred, and slowly he found the new angles, the necessary approaches, the blocks that would conserve his effort.

By the time they stopped, his left shoulder hurt. He'd demanded a greater range from it today than he had in years. He reached up to squeeze it, remembering too late he didn't have a hand to do so.

Arthur's sword thumped to the ground. "Here." Before Bedwyr could move, Arthur's hands were on his shoulder.

Bedwyr opened his mouth to tell him off…then shut it. They felt too good, those hands. They looked like his father Matthias's, long-fingered and square, and they were strong. He closed his eyes briefly, unwilling to give anything away when the lad was standing so close, smelling of sun-warmed effort. But when the hands began to shift up, toward Bedwyr's neck, he stepped away. "That'll do."

He was halfway to the water jug when he realized he hadn't reciprocated.

And that he couldn't.

~

He watched Arthur build up the fire again that night. The flames made his hair look as though it were on fire as well. He wore it long, like most in the village, but where some men let theirs hang loose,

Arthur kept his hair tied back. It was something Bedwyr had always found odd about him. Arthur was cockier than the plain, neat queue of hair implied. And the color, while not exactly rare, was unusual. He'd heard more than one woman comment on it. If Arthur would let it loose, he might have his pick of the more game among them.

"Too warm?"

Bedwyr jolted, realized he'd been staring. "No, it's fine."

He lay back and glared at the roof beams while Arthur stripped to sleep. Even avoiding the sight, he was aware of how the fire made the other man's skin glow; it lit the hut as well as a lantern. When Arthur stretched, he sent long shadows against the walls and thatching. Finally his shadow bent, and he crawled into his bedding.

Bedwyr let go of a tight breath.

When he'd woken this morning, he'd wanted nothing more than to get rid of his eager guest. He supposed Arthur felt guilty for his conduct in the skirmish. At dawn, the notion of the lad's guilt had seemed irrelevant; the damage had been done. Bedwyr wouldn't fight again. He wouldn't lead. He would live the rest of his days alone and pitied, by himself as much as others.

Those things were still true. But maybe...maybe he could put off the loneliness for a few days more.

It grated to admit it, but Arthur was fair company. His guilt was a burden Bedwyr didn't want, and he hoped the cub would give up any outrageous hopes he might have of restoring Bedwyr to his former level of skill. He would practice, and perhaps he might be able to defend himself in an emergency. Mostly, though, it was good not to be the only body in the hut.

His traitorous mind pointed out that Arthur's was a particularly fine body, of all the possibilities in their village. Only a couple others had ever caught Bedwyr's eye, and none of them were likely to avail themselves to him.

He might as well enjoy the view while he could.

Arthur shifted on the floor, and Bedwyr wondered if he should give up the bed. But after another stretch and a sigh, Arthur settled on his back, seemingly comfortable.

Still, it was cold...

Say goodnight, fool. You don't want to sleep on the floor.

The only person he ever bid a good night was his sister, and she usually said it to him first and then punctuated it with a kiss to his forehead. He could only imagine the expression on Arthur's face if he were to do such a thing. Not that he would, but it was amusing to ponder.

In the end, he aimed for a compliment.

"It was a good idea you had, to discard the shields."

Arthur looked at him. "Seemed best."

Who was this understated person? He almost missed the more boisterous lad Arthur usually was. "We'll do the same tomorrow."

The contour of Arthur's face changed as he smiled. "All right."

Bedwyr felt his own face heating under Arthur's scrutiny and was glad the light was dim. "Good night."

"Fire bright."

"What?"

"What? Oh." Arthur gave what sounded like an embarrassed chuckle. "Habit. Something my grandfather used to say."

"Master Wolf?"

"Yeah."

The old smith. Bedwyr could imagine him blessing his grandchildren with the words. "Tomorrow then."

"Tomorrow."

Huh.

Bedwyr lay back and watched the beam shadows twitch overhead.

Tomorrow.

Now there was something he hadn't thought he'd anticipate again.

CHAPTER 7

When the bed frame creaked behind him, Arthur thought it was his own joints. Then Bedwyr snuffled and groaned, and Arthur smiled to himself. Bending to the hearth again, he blew the coals to life, feeding the tinder with a few sticks. They wouldn't need a large fire this morning, not if he could get his charge out of the hut and sparring as quickly as he meant to.

Satisfied the fire would tend itself for the time being, he rose and pulled his shirt from the rafter beam. The wool brushed his skin coolly for a few seconds, sending a shiver across his back. Rolling his shoulders to ease it brought yesterday's aches to the surface.

He hadn't trained weak-handed in a long time. It was one of the things his grandfather had insisted on but Lord Uthyr had scorned. Why should a man waste his time doing such a thing when he could be building his gods-gifted strengths?

Strange that they found themselves here now, in exactly the sort of situation Grandfather had said men must prepare for, and that Lord Uthyr had sent Arthur here to practice the Roman's way of things. He wondered if Lord Uthyr felt any remorse for prodding Grandfather about his methods—or if Grandfather was having a great laugh from beyond.

Crossing to the table, he laid out four bannocks from Gwen's cloth and spread a thick, creamy layer of cheese on each. Stuffing one in his mouth and palming another, he grabbed the water pail and slipped out of the hut.

The air was chill outside. After a quick piss, he walked to the stream and knelt to fill the pail. Just as the vessel grew heavy, a flash upstream caught his attention, the briefest glimpse of a silvery tail. The sight felt like another gift. Getting a basket of food from Gwen every day was nice, but grown men could feed themselves. He made a mental note of the fish's location, then carried the water back to the hut.

Bedwyr had dressed and stood before the table, holding one of the bannocks.

"Morning," Arthur said.

"Morning." Bedwyr bit into the bannock.

"Brought water if you want some."

A grunt and another big bite.

"Saw a fish in the stream. I'll make a trap later."

Bedwyr nodded and reached for the second bannock.

"Grandfather taught Cai and me to make them. Cai's better at it, but it's not alchemy. You just need some green twigs—"

"Do you always talk so much in the morning?"

He closed his mouth at Bedwyr's grouchy scowl. Rolling up his bedding, he tidied the hearth area. He couldn't afford to get himself tossed out. He had a few fine lines to walk here, between drawing Bedwyr out and giving him peace, between feeding him and coddling him, between building up his confidence and causing discouragement. He wanted to do all of the former and more, but Bedwyr was still strong enough to shove him out the door. He was proud.

But while pride could be injured, it could be prodded too, and Arthur wasn't above using that. Taking up his sword, he gave the man's left shoulder a solid clap on his way past.

Bedwyr half shouted in pain.

Arthur tipped his head. "Sorry, are you sore?" He rotated his own left arm, as if checking for pain, then shrugged, as if the ache in it weren't already pulsing. "Must be my youth."

Bedwyr shook his head and retrieved his sword from where it leaned on the wall. "Let's go, cub."

Despite their belligerent start, they settled into a measured session. Keeping a close eye on the other man's expression and posture, gauging them for fatigue or useless frustration, Arthur paced their sparring with breaks he claimed he needed himself.

And sometimes he did need them. He'd goaded Bedwyr enough

to fuel true effort, even if it had as its impetus a desire to put Arthur down. That was fine with him; whatever kept Bedwyr at it, kept him trying, was a tactic Arthur was willing to exploit.

As it had been the day before, their parries were as awkward as ducks lighting on solid ground. But the ground *was* solid, and so were Bedwyr and his lifetime of training. As the morning warmed marginally toward midday, there came a shift. Arthur couldn't point to its beginning—only recognized it in progress—but it brought his first real spark of hope. At some moment while they sparred, Bedwyr wrested control of his sword from whatever force had been standing in his path. Though not graceful, his subsequent strikes carried more intention. He began to follow through on his swings, lending them greater power. Using their weak hands was forcing their entire bodies to reset, to push off and lead with feet unaccustomed to doing each other's work, and to not throw what had been their shield shoulders into the fight.

After a couple of hours, sweat had soaked their shirts. Arthur's weak arm burned with fatigue. A certain tightness around Bedwyr's eyes said he felt the same. When Arthur waved his sword in a wobbly arc toward the stream, Bedwyr nodded.

At the shallow bank, Arthur stripped his shirt and straddled the small creek. The water felt just as cold as it had that morning, leaving his face tingling. Hoping to encourage Bedwyr to do the same, he scooped the frigid water into his hands and splashed it onto his chest. He yelped involuntarily as it slid down his belly and into his breeches.

Bedwyr chuckled—a sound Arthur tried not to focus too intently on—and his shirt landed on the snowy bank. His boots planted themselves at the creek's edges, and then his big hand was hauling water up and against his body.

Arthur tried not to watch, truly. But the way Bed's hand moved over his chest was, well, fascinating. His fingers pushing through his hair, parting it so that Arthur could see the blue-black lines of the tattoos hidden underneath. He watched them move as Bedwyr washed himself and huffed at the cold water. When that water coursed down Bedwyr's furry belly to dampen the front of his breeches, Arthur grabbed his shirt and dunked it, wringing it out hastily, and then stepped out of the stream. He was clean enough. Stopping in the hut just long enough to don his dry shirt and hang his wet one, he fled again to make his fish trap.

By midafternoon, one of the stream's fish had generously swum into the long basket he'd fashioned and fixed underwater. Unable to back out of it, the fat, shiny creature had settled in, floating and awaiting rescue.

Unfortunately for the fish, rescue involved a thorough gutting and scaling, and soon Arthur found himself bent over another fire, this one in an old pit whose depression he'd spotted in the snow behind the hut. He nurtured it to a low but steady heat and then spitted the fish to cook over it.

When the fish was nearly ready, he went to find Bedwyr. He was unduly excited about presenting the man with a roasted trout and tried to contain the stupid grin he surely wore. But it unfurled again when Bedwyr followed him 'round the hut and barked in surprise at the sizzling treat.

"From the stream?"

"Yeah."

"Catch it with your hands?"

Arthur stopped mid-kneel next to the spit. "With a trap."

"Oh." Bedwyr shrugged as if disappointed. "Just thought with your *youth* and all…"

An unexpected arrow of pleasure shot through Arthur's middle at the teasing, tangling his thoughts. "Should be done."

It was a meager meal, shared between them, but the crispy skin and flaky flesh, combined with Bedwyr's rumbling enjoyment of both, made it a feast. When he'd finished, Bedwyr tossed the bones into the fire and sucked his fingers clean, one by one.

Arthur resolved to trap two fish next time.

Finishing off his own half, he quickly rose and put another log on the fire. It felt right to share a campfire. He sat, watching the flames and trying to conjure something to talk about.

"Sore?"

Arthur looked up at Bedwyr's question, then realized he'd been rubbing his left shoulder. "Yeah," he admitted. "Yours?"

"No," Bedwyr said, then gave him a sheepish smile. "It fucking *hurts*."

Arthur laughed. Gods, but he wanted to touch him, to work the pain from him. He settled for commiserating. "Good day's work, I suppose."

"I suppose." Bedwyr squinted and rotated his arm.

Arthur hesitated, but then decided there could be no harm in asking. "Did you feel the shift?"

Bedwyr stopped and looked at him. "Shift?"

"In your control. Your stance."

"No." He looked at Arthur, curious.

He should tread lightly here. No need to pile it on, as much as he might want to. Bedwyr would think that a friendly lie. "Happened in the second hour. Your strikes grew more…" What word wouldn't insult what his strikes had been beforehand?

"Confident?" Bedwyr said.

Arthur studied him, trying to suss his reaction.

"Well?"

"Yes."

Bedwyr nodded and turned back to the fire. He sat quietly for a long moment, elbows on his knees. "I want you to tell me."

"Tell you what?"

"Anything you notice." Bedwyr looked at him. "Good or bad."

"Promise not to throttle me for it?"

"No."

Arthur sat still, as trapped in the man's dark gaze as a trout in a wicker basket. Then Bedwyr's expression cracked into a smile again.

Without thinking, Arthur scooped up a handful of snow and chucked it at Bedwyr's head. He missed.

Bedwyr didn't.

"Good aim," Arthur said, wiping snow from his hair.

Bedwyr chuckled and turned to the fire. "Good target."

Arthur's treacherous belly performed a somersault. He held his hands to the fire's heat to keep them from joining in the mutiny.

~ ~ ~

They ate together in the mornings and began training soon after.

For a full cycle of the moon, they left their shields in the hut, concentrating on sword craft. It was difficult but becoming less so. Bedwyr used his short arm for balance in these matches; he couldn't remember now when he'd stopped feeling self-conscious about it. It simply was, and in unshielded sparring it was no more or less useful than his left arm had been before his injury.

By the time midday rolled in, though, their clothes were always sweat-soaked despite the cold, and his stump throbbed. At that point, they broke. He would go to the creek to bathe his chest and back. Sitting on the bank, he'd hold his short arm under the chilly water as long as he could stand to. Some days the throb made it seem as though his hand were still there, unseen, and numbing the skin helped.

Arthur never joined him at the creek, choosing instead to collect firewood or check the snares he'd laid in the surrounding hills for rabbits. Bedwyr supposed he should be thankful, and he was, but sometimes he found himself wanting to continue their sparring at the creek, swords or no.

Some days, Gwen appeared with her food basket while Arthur was still out.

"You look hale," she said today.

"I feel hale," he admitted.

"Yes?" She glanced at his sword, where it leaned against the wall near the hut's door. "Are you training?"

He played it down, lest she want to see for herself. "Not training. Only learning to use it left-handed."

"That's training, big brother."

"It's what I say it is, little sister."

She made a grumpy face at him. "You're eating better."

"That's Arthur. He eats half my share."

She grinned at him. "So take it back."

"I don't need it. He does."

"And why is that?"

"Growing lad and all that."

"Oh, and you're past those days." She gave him an elbow to the ribs. "A full-grown man, are you?"

Nothing stole the bluster from a fellow as quickly as mockery from a sister. "Shut up."

"Good response. Very mature."

There was nothing he could say that wouldn't sound even more petulant.

"I'll pack more tomorrow."

"Don't." At her look, he shrugged. "You shouldn't have to feed us. We're capable."

She looked about the hut and its hearth, bare of implements or pots.

"He catches fish."

"Arthur?"

He nodded.

"Which you cook…"

"Outside. There's a fire pit around the back."

She still looked skeptical, but relented. "All right." She continued to empty the basket. "Is there anything you'd like from Master Matthias?"

"No."

She glanced up. "Really?"

His response had been automatic, a knee-jerk denial of need, but now that he had a chance to consider, he knew it had been true as well. "The arm's healing fine. Tell him that. There's only pain if we train too hard."

She smiled. "So you *are* training."

"What's in that?" he asked, pointing to one of two parcels wrapped in cloth.

Gwen squinted at him to let him know she recognized his diversion. "It's sweet cake."

He perked up. "You don't say."

She blocked him bodily from the cake. "Oat bread first."

Stooping, he tipped her over his shoulder. He hadn't done so since she was a girl. He missed it.

Perhaps she didn't, the way she shrieked and beat his back with her hands. Grinning to himself as she carried on, he unwrapped one of the parcels. The cloth came away sticky with honey. He scraped a finger through it and tasted. "Mmm."

Gwen kicked. "Food first!"

"Sweet cake is food." He clamped down on her legs with his stump and picked up the cake.

"Put me down!"

"No." He took a big bite. The familiar nutty sweetness made him groan.

"Oaf!"

"What's going on in here?"

He turned at Arthur's voice, swinging Gwen in an arc that made her squeal.

Arthur crossed his arms, taking in the scene with a smirk. "Hullo, Gwen."

"Tell him to set me down!"

"She brought cake," Bedwyr told him around a mouthful.

Arthur's copper eyebrows rose. "Cake?"

"Sweet cake."

"I like sweet cake."

"There's a second one."

"And oat bread, Arthur," Gwen said in an imperious tone despite being upside-down. "Good, wholesome oat bread, and cheese, and apples."

"Ohhh." Arthur nodded at him. "She expected you to eat those first."

Bedwyr scoffed in mutual disbelief.

"No such luck," Arthur agreed. "Where's this cake?"

"Enjoy it," Gwen said. "It'll be the last I bring you."

"You don't mean that," Arthur mumbled, his mouth full. He grinned at Bedwyr as Gwen renewed her flailing.

When they'd eaten all but a bite, he set her on her feet. She scowled at them red-faced. Bedwyr silently offered her the last morsel, and she snatched it. "Boors."

"Thank you, Gwen," they said in unison.

Rolling her eyes, she gathered her basket and huffed toward the door. "Eat the rest or it'll be fish for you, day in and out." She shot him a glare, but he could see the fondness behind it.

When she left, Arthur reached for an apple.

"Spar?" Bedwyr said.

Arthur stilled and looked up, surprised. "Again? You don't want to eat?"

"Just did."

Arthur nodded. "All right then."

CHAPTER 8

The air outside felt good on Bedwyr's face. The hut was a touch small for three grown bodies. Gripping his sword, he turned to face Arthur.

"I wager she makes another one," Arthur said and struck.

Bedwyr knocked his blade to the side. "Another what?"

"Sweet cake."

"You'll lose that wager. That was the last, she said."

Arthur feinted to the left. "How about this wager then: *when* she brings another sweet cake, winner gets it."

Bedwyr swung, connecting hard. "Winner? Of what?"

"This." Arthur lunged, and Bedwyr dodged, just. "Today."

"Worth risking humiliation, is it?"

"Yours, yes," Arthur said and licked his lower lip.

Bedwyr's gaze snagged on the tip of tongue and nearly missed the next strike. "Keep dreaming, cub." He landed a blow that pushed a grunt from the other man. "I'll eat it in front of you, then suck my fingers clean."

Arthur muttered something under his breath and swung. The force of it rang up Bedwyr's arm, and he laughed.

When was the last time this had been fun? He and Cai had fought well together and had celebrated victories. But when had been the last time he'd laughed while sparring? Had he ever? As a boy, maybe. Away from the scrutiny of his father or Master Marcus, of course. He'd wanted too badly to be the perfect warrior, the rightful heir to his father's domain—for them to see him as such—to let down his guard around them.

But this. This was something else altogether. Out of sight of anyone who had any expectations of him, he was...enjoying himself. Was that even reasonable? He had one hand and was trying to learn to take down another man without its mate. No, reason had no place here. No reasonable man would have begun to imagine, over the past days, that he might be able to come back into the esteem of his father after falling from it so spectacularly. But he had thought about that, and the smallest kernel of hope had taken root deep in his chest. Shouting as if battle-mad, he charged Arthur.

Arthur fell back a step, thrown off by Bedwyr's greater weight, but then braced himself on his long legs and pushed. He drove Bedwyr backward with a wicked series of strikes that had him thinking of nothing but how to fend off each blow as it came, unable to anticipate the next. Arthur was quick, and surprising. He tried angles and approaches Bedwyr didn't expect, forcing him to treat every swing as imperative. He gave Bedwyr no quarter, no halfhearted parries during which to catch his breath.

That Bedwyr was still laughing didn't help matters.

"I'm winning, by the way," Arthur said.

"Are not."

"Gods, you gasp like an old man."

Bedwyr growled and threw himself forward. He was swinging wildly, but so was Arthur. Their clashes rang in the cold air. *Old man.* He'd show this cub. He'd show the hills and the sky too, and any gods bored enough to watch. He'd held a sword since his fourth birth celebration. He was Bedwyr ap Uthyr and grandson of Emrys. He was a warrior of Cymru, and no people were fiercer—

Unless one slipped on a patch of muddy earth and landed squarely on one's recently amputated arm.

He clenched his teeth as pain flashed up his limb and across his chest. When its claws eased slightly, he risked a breath. Pushing to his feet before he was ready, because he could feel Arthur watching him, he straightened on shaky knees.

"Water," he said, then pointed at Arthur. "Wager's moot. Gwen's too stubborn to bring another cake."

Arthur smiled, his teeth bright against his flushed face. "We'll see."

Bedwyr tamped the urge to knock him down. Holding himself

tightly in check, he headed to the stream.

But he thought about it as he drank, about all the ways one might trip another man backward, trap his gangly arms and legs under one's own, and shut his cocksure mouth.

~ ~ ~

When Bedwyr made for the stream, Arthur veered in a different direction. The hut was too small to contain his restlessness, and the stream was out of the question. He'd gone once, early on, but the sight of Bedwyr's bare, wet chest had made his hands itch. Now, just seeing the man's beard dripping with water would erode the last of Arthur's will not to touch him. He spent the next two hours gathering fuel for a fire and trying to calm his thoughts.

Bedwyr was healing. More than that, he was learning to use his sword, and well. Arthur would suggest they take up their shields again, maybe on the morrow. The more he could put between Bedwyr's body and his own, the better.

This afternoon had been a special trial: Bedwyr, laughing.

Arthur had seen him do it, of course, quietly, in the way he did everything but fight. He'd heard it enough as a boy, when Cai and Bedwyr were getting up to something or enjoying a joke. He'd seen it at the story fire sometimes; the man enjoyed a good tale as much as anyone else. Even on the way to meet the Saxons, Bedwyr's campfire laugh had been a subdued compared to the other men.

Today, he'd laughed loudly. It had taken Arthur by surprise the first time. In fact, he hadn't thought it a laugh so much as a triumphant *ha* sort of sound. But when he'd glanced at Bedwyr's face, he'd been smiling, and not the sweet smile Arthur had developed a secret taste for, but an openmouthed, panting grin. It had etched lines at the corners of Bedwyr's eyes and dimples into his cheeks just above his thick beard. Arthur had stared a moment too long, and Bedwyr had taken advantage and driven him back several paces.

Arthur hadn't wanted it to stop. Against his better judgment, he'd quickened his attacks, made them as unpredictable as possible, purely because they set Bedwyr off, until his laughter had become hoarse in ways that made Arthur wonder what he might sound like if—

He halted and dropped the firewood on the ground.

Grandpapa Wolf had done this when he was a boy and making

trouble in the smithy. His grandfather would up-end a jar of nails onto the ground, and Arthur had to pick them up and put them back into the jar, one at a time, and put his thoughts in order as he did so.

These thoughts he was having now would lead nowhere but to frustration. For the next few minutes, he concentrated on picking up the pieces of firewood, one by one, deliberately.

Gather it, he told himself. *Take it back. Start a fire.*

And nothing else.

When he returned to the hut, Bedwyr was sitting on a stump outside. Arthur's traitorous eyes looked for signs of Bedwyr's wash and found them in the dampness at the open neck of his shirt and the shine of the dark hair over his forehead, where he'd smoothed it with his hand. His head was bent to a stone he held in the crook of his short arm, using it to whet his dagger with short, sharp strokes.

"You'll slice your arm off."

He almost tripped when he realized what he'd said, but Bedwyr only raised an eyebrow at him. "Too late."

Arthur dumped his firewood on the stack and ducked into the hut before he could make a bigger fool of himself.

He built a small fire and warmed the stew Gwen had brought. Bedwyr came inside after a while, his dagger sheathed at his belt again.

"What kind is it?"

"Rabbit, I think."

Bedwyr hummed. "She makes good rabbit."

"We should be feeding ourselves."

"I told her the same. She must enjoy it."

Arthur looked at him. "You think?"

Bedwyr shrugged. "Why else would she do it?"

"To see you?"

Bedwyr scoffed, then gave Arthur a speculative look. "To see you, maybe."

Arthur shook his head and turned back to the stew.

"No?"

"No."

"You could do worse," Bedwyr said defensively.

"I know that."

Bedwyr was quiet for a moment, then made a dismissive sound. "She'll be married off for alliance anyway."

Thankfully, he let it go after that. Arthur divided the hot stew between two bowls, and they ate in silence.

Afterward, they sat on their respective stools and watched the low flame dance above the coals. Outside, the daylight grew rosy, and then dimmed to night. Neither of them moved to light a lantern, but Arthur put another stick on the fire. It was just enough to allow him to see the contours of Bedwyr's face.

Presently, they formed a frown, and he pressed a thumb into his shoulder.

Arthur's resolve crumbled. "Let me."

Bedwyr didn't protest, so Arthur laid his hands on the large knot of muscle that made up Bedwyr's left shoulder. He squeezed it through the wool of his shirt, and the man groaned.

"Sore?"

"Yeah."

He massaged his shoulder, digging in with his thumbs. He took his time, savoring every sound that grated from Bedwyr's throat. And the warmth. It radiated through Bedwyr's shirt, taking off the chill that the hut and his own nerves had set in his fingers. He welcomed the heat into his hands, could almost feel it stealing up his arms and into his chest, wrapping his knock-about heart in a soothing cloak. He drank it up like hot, spiced ale at the solstice because Bedwyr might stop him at any moment, might pull away and end the contact, as he'd done outside.

Except he didn't. Not when Arthur eased down to his forearm. Or when he stood and gripped the muscles on either side of Bedwyr's neck and worked the tension from those. Or when he moved to his right shoulder.

Instead, Bedwyr sat quietly, watching the fire, and let him continue.

So he did.

After treating his shoulder thoroughly, he rubbed down that arm as well, spending several minutes above his elbow, trying to guess how the man might react if he continued down his forearm.

He took a chance and squeezed lower. Bedwyr's arm hung loosely by his side. As he worked, Arthur studied Bedwyr's profile, looking for signs of…well, anything. No sign appeared until he neared the end, and Bedwyr squinted.

Arthur eased up his pressure. "Is there pain?" His voice sounded raspy in the hush, as if he needed to clear his throat.

Bedwyr turned and met his eyes for a long moment. "Only at the stump."

Arthur rolled up Bedwyr's sleeve to expose his arm. Tentatively, he cupped the stump. The skin there was cooler than the rest of Bedwyr's skin. It felt gnarled. He gave it a light squeeze, and Bedwyr's arm jerked.

He looked up to find dark eyes watching him. Holding their gaze, he gave another squeeze.

Bedwyr's mouth dropped open, and he exhaled slowly. His eyelids fell shut.

"All right?"

Bedwyr swallowed but nodded.

He spent a few minutes on the arm, kneading the scar with his fingertips. Bedwyr's expression shifted in the firelight, his brow letting go of its stern set as if Arthur were smoothing the lines there with his thumb. He wondered what it would be like to touch the man's face but couldn't think of even a far-fetched reason to do so.

As if he'd heard Arthur's thoughts, Bedwyr opened his eyes.

Arthur let him go, crossing his arms to hide his restless fists.

Bedwyr looked at him and smiled. "Thanks."

Arthur nodded, trusting his voice no more than he trusted his hands.

~

He woke in the night to a touch on his shoulder. When he opened his eyes, Bedwyr was only a shadow against the dark shapes of the beams overhead.

"Wh-what is it?" As soon as he said it, his body shuddered.

"I can hear your fucking teeth chattering. Come on."

"Where?"

"Into bed."

The shiver that racked him then had nothing to do with the cold. Bedwyr had to be joking.

The blankets covering him were swept away, bringing on another shiver. He wasn't joking.

Heart ticking in his ears, Arthur stood and picked up the blankets he'd been lying on. Cautiously he shuffled toward the bed.

"Ease in, the thing's ancient."

He followed Bedwyr's voice down until his hand touched the edge of the wooden frame.

"Maybe I should stay on the floor—"

"Get in the bed, man."

Before he could second-guess himself anymore, he lay down on his side, as close to the edge of the mattress as possible. It gave way under him with small crunching sounds. He should have smelled the ticking's old, dry grass but instead the scent of Bedwyr's skin teased his nose. With shaking hands, he spread the last two blankets over them before settling.

One big arm came over his waist and hauled him back into Bedwyr's body.

Arthur exhaled, a harsh sound in the dark. "You're warm."

"That's the point."

The words licked at the back of his neck. He was pressed against the thick muscle of Bedwyr's chest. How many times had he wanted this? He could have filled a scroll with the scenarios he fantasized about. Bedwyr crooking a finger to draw him across the hot pool in the forest. Pinning him to the dirt in the training yard. Pushing him to kneel.

When it came to lying down, his usual imagining had them nose to nose and legs tangled, as if one of them had just tripped the other. He hadn't really considered the particular benefits of the position he found himself in now. Bedwyr's shoulders were broader than his own, so that the man's heat surrounded him. His belly pushed into Arthur's back unapologetically. Best of all, at some point in the past couple of weeks, Bedwyr had stopped sleeping in his trousers. Arthur didn't know what the man had had to be shy about—nothing, to his mind. Seeing him lie down half-clothed had only served to inspire more fantasies in which Arthur plucked the laces loose and stripped the breeches away inch by agonizing inch.

The only problem now, and something else he hadn't anticipated, was that the soft fur of Bedwyr's body tickled him in a thousand maddening places.

"Stop wriggling."

He forced himself to lie still. His breath puffed before him, stuttering as his chills slowly eased. Under his head, Bedwyr's biceps flexed as he made an adjustment. It was his short arm. "Am I hurting you?"

"No."

Bedwyr's hand rested on the mattress, the curl of his knuckles brushing Arthur's belly as he breathed. If he didn't calm himself, his cock would soon be nudging the man's fist for attention. He shifted. "I'm taller. I should go behind—ah!"

He gulped back the gasp, immobilized. After a few seconds, Bedwyr's fingers released his nipple. Blood flowed into it again, leaving it throbbing.

Hot breath brushed his ear. "Cub?"

The nickname, growled in a low, warning tone, sent blood rushing into his prick. "Yeah?"

"Go to sleep."

Arthur closed his eyes.

Start a fire. Nothing else.

Too late.

CHAPTER 9

Arthur woke to a powerful snore.

Behind him, Bedwyr lay on his back. Arthur smiled that a fellow who lived his days so quietly would make such a racket in his sleep. He hadn't snored like this when Arthur first arrived, which made him wonder if Bedwyr had truly slept. Maybe it was just their training; they tended to spar to exhaustion for want of anything else to do. Even so, it had taken him a long time to fall back to sleep after Bedwyr had cajoled him into the bed several nights before.

The murky dawn light always gave him the sense of being in a cave. In this protected space, the world outside might have ceased to exist for all Bedwyr seemed concerned about it. His brow was relaxed so that he looked younger than usual, as if there weren't four years between them.

There were, but did they mean so much?

He watched Bedwyr's chest rise and fall on several breaths, and then he left the warmth of the bed to dress, as he'd done every morning since sharing it with Bedwyr. This morning, though, he wasn't bent on chores. The thoughts crowding his mind had become too tangled to sort on his own. He needed help; today he would seek it. After packing an apple and a hunk of cheese in a sack, he slipped out the door as quietly as he could.

It took him an hour to reach his destination. If he hadn't known the way so well, the snow might have put him off until spring. The sky lightened as he forged a path through the hills and valleys, from deep blue to gray to pink and then daylight. It was clear, the air crisp enough to nip at his ears. As he kicked through the snow, he tried to gather his thoughts so he'd be ready to share them when he arrived.

The hill was as steep as always. By the time he reached the top, he was breathing hard and his thighs trembled. He put a hand to the stone, palm flat and fingers spread, before lowering himself onto the ground to sit against the rock.

"Good morning."

He smiled as he imagined the response. It would have rumbled like the thunder that rolled through their valleys sometimes.

It *was* a good morning, at least as far as the view was concerned. In the distance to the west, the sea rippled. He'd never touched it, that water. Word was that it was salty, and that he had been born within feet of such water, but then his people had carried their belongings and their lives into the mountains and settled there because it was safer.

So much for safety.

"Bedwyr lost his hand to a Saxon." He didn't want to say the next part, but this had always been a place for speaking truth. "It was my fault."

He waited, breath held, even though he didn't expect a reply. The stone at his back was solid and cool. Impassive. It encouraged him to keep talking.

"Papa stitched him up, and there was no corruption. Bedwyr's lucky, I think. Other men have died from injuries like that."

He didn't know what he would have done if Bedwyr had died. Seemed silly to voice such a thing, even here, where he could do so without reprimand. Silly because it hadn't happened, so why dwell on it? The important thing was now.

"It was his sword hand. I've been helping him learn how to fight with his other hand. It was hard at first. We left off with the shields, and we've been sparring with only our blades for a month." He rubbed a fingertip over the new calluses on his left palm. "We should probably take up the shields again. Mama outfitted his with extra bindings, so he could use it on his short arm."

A falcon circled overhead, looking for prey. Finding none, it wheeled into the adjacent valley.

He'd been ten years old when he'd tattooed himself to impress Bedwyr. It was a crude thing, the blue-black figure on his left arm, not remotely impressive. Grandpapa Wolf had been the only one to recognize his motivation and had sat with him, answering questions he hadn't known he'd had. Questions that seemed to multiply as he grew older. The smith had always been there for him.

"You told me once I could talk to you about him. About Bedwyr." He picked at the dry grass at the base of the rock. "It's like a pain, isn't it?"

The falcon cried out.

"I mean, a pain that's not pain, exactly. It happens when I see him. When he talks to me. When we fight. Sometimes it's like when you strike something wrong and it rings up your arm and makes you shout. Other times it's as if he's tied a rope around my chest and is tightening it and pulling me toward him at the same time. Do you know that feeling?"

He looked for the falcon, but it had flown on.

"*Did* you know that feeling?"

The stone at his back remained still.

But he'd known it would.

This had been their place, this spot high on the hill with an occasional view of the sea. Around the time of his ill-conceived tattoo, his grandfathers had begun to come here. It had been a cave then, and Grandfather Marcus had fitted it out so that he and Grandpapa Wolf could spend the night inside. It was sheltered by the tall, broad stone at his back and had been accessible by a large crack in the rock.

He had followed them once, and then come back alone to investigate. There'd been a sort of bed built into the ground inside. The grass that made up its ticking had crackled under him, and its dry scent helped him doze off. He'd almost overslept and had woken in just enough time to run home in the waning daylight.

As a boy, he'd had a difficult time imagining what they did at the cave; neither was prone to sitting idle. Now, though, sharing the small hut with Bedwyr, he understood at least part of what had drawn them here.

They had loved him, and Cai and Mora, but they never offered to bring any of them here, even when Mora had begged. It had been theirs alone. When they passed, it had remained theirs. The great crack in the stone was filled, and the blackberry brambles that grew up either side were allowed to climb and cross and tangle until only the small bit of stone against which he sat now remained clear, with help from him, whenever he visited.

The old smith *had* known the feeling he spoke of, that sense of binding. Arthur had seen it in his eyes whenever he'd looked at Grandfather Marcus. As if he would have followed him anywhere. By all accounts, he had done just that—across Gaul, across the sea, across Britannia and Cymru, and then across these hills many times—right to this place.

Wolf had known it, that pulling. It had never seemed to make him weaker. If anything it had trained him into the strongest man Arthur had known.

Except maybe for one other. Over the past few weeks, Bedwyr had surpassed Arthur's hopes. He suspected Bedwyr had been fighting two opponents: Arthur, for certain, but also a voice inside that said *give up*. Sometimes during a sparring session, Bedwyr's eyes seemed not so much focused on Arthur's sword as on that voice. Seeing him like that spurred Arthur to draw the man back out—back to him—so that the moment Bedwyr's eyes lit on him with recognition…

Arthur could no longer deny it: he wanted nothing else. No one else. He wanted to see that spark of knowing every time Bedwyr looked at him, wanted to give it back to him until he understood the potential, their potential. They had a place like this one to explore it.

But he would have to make the first strike.

"Thanks for listening, Papa Wolf."

He knocked his fists against the stone, then rose and headed back to the hut.

~ ~ ~

Arthur came strolling back to the hut midmorning.

Bedwyr had woken to an empty room. The banked fire had let the air cool to a chill. Most mornings, Arthur stirred the coals to heat the space, but he hadn't been there when Bedwyr opened his eyes.

At first, he'd been glad of it, glad to have a private moment to put on a neutral mask. Being curled around Arthur's long body the past several nights had begun to fire something he'd tried to quell for a long time. It waited in him like a grate stacked with tinder and fuel. All it needed was the spark of one stone colliding with another. Which of them was the iron and which the brittle flint?

But then he'd had a couple of hours to doubt that Arthur would want to be either instrument. They'd shared a bed, was all, because the nights were frozen. He hadn't planned to touch Arthur, let alone pinch him that first time. Arthur certainly hadn't expected it. While his reaction had fed the hidden flame inside Bedwyr like a bellows, perhaps there'd been nothing more to it than reasonable shock. Arthur escaped as soon as daylight broke every morning.

By the time Arthur appeared over the edge of the hillside midmorning, Bedwyr had worked himself into a tight ball of uncertainty. Unable to discern any clues from the cub's expression or posture, he jumped up and grabbed their swords, eager to lose his churning thoughts in the physical work of practice.

A few strikes in, he became aware of something different. It wasn't himself, or not completely—he hadn't improved that much. Nor had Arthur, though he fought more aggressively this morning. Arthur didn't seem as calm as he had for the past weeks. Even when his swings had grown playful and unpredictable before, he'd always carried through with an easy confidence that had been infectious and forgiving of Bedwyr's own struggle. His movements were difficult to predict today too, but a thread of something else ran through them.

By the second hour of practice, Bedwyr was certain of it. It pervaded their temporary training yard, the sense that Arthur had somehow caught a bolt of lightning and held it inside. Bedwyr was drawn to him, as if his body craved destruction.

They picked at the leftovers from the basket Gwen had brought a few days before, and then they passed a muted afternoon, circling each other in the routine of chores they had settled into. The tugging sensation remained, raising the short hairs on Bedwyr's neck. More than once, he stopped what he was doing to study the sky, but it was unusually clear.

It was going to be another cold night.

~

Arthur joined him in the bed without prompting, for which Bedwyr was grateful. If he'd had to maneuver Arthur into it again tonight, it would have come out as an order or as a plea, and he didn't want either. He wanted him to do it of his own volition, even if it only meant he didn't want to sleep on the ground anymore.

He edged back to the wall to make room. The old wooden frame creaked under Arthur's weight, and then he was there, his head resting on Bedwyr's short arm. He was long enough that his arse rested against Bedwyr's thighs instead of in his lap, which was probably for the best. His hair smelled of smoke and sweat. Bedwyr laid his other arm benignly over Arthur's side, let his hand rest on the bed. What would it be like to rub his knuckles on Arthur's belly?

He curled his fingers safely into a fist. "Good spar today."

Arthur nodded. "It was."

And with that, Bedwyr exhausted his cache of prepared words. He didn't want to sleep yet, though. Rather, he didn't want Arthur to sleep yet. "Where did you go this morning?"

Gods, but that sounded needful.

"To my grandfathers' tomb."

Not the response he'd expected. "You go often?"

Arthur shrugged against him. "Now and then. Papa Wolf..." Arthur grunted, and Bedwyr wondered if the nickname embarrassed him. "He was, uh...easy to talk to."

"Your grandfather Marcus was not."

Arthur laughed. It sounded good in the quiet hut, felt even better against Bedwyr's chest. "He was more demanding," Arthur said. "No coddling from Grandfather."

"He was patient with me."

"Marcus Roman, patient?" He shook his head on Bedwyr's arm. "No one ever accused him of that."

Bedwyr supposed they hadn't. In his memory, the man was always moving—demonstrating a tactic, circling the training yard, maintaining the weaponry in the armory. But anyone who hadn't seen past the Roman's physical restlessness hadn't been paying attention. Marcus's focus during training had been total, and he'd insisted on the same effort from his charges. Sometimes it seemed they had to repeat the same maneuver half the day before the old man was satisfied. "He trained Cai and me together. We probably pushed him to the end of his tether every fucking day."

"Well, sure, *Cai* did. But Grandfather never had anything contrary to say about you. In fact, he told Cai more than once he should strive to be more like you."

Such was the influence Master Marcus had had on him that Bedwyr swelled with pride at that.

"Fired Cai like a torch every time."

Bedwyr laughed. "I wager it did. He'd rather emulate my father."

"Exactly. Which infuriated Grandfather."

"No love lost?"

Arthur went still.

Hiding behind friendly banter, Bedwyr knocked his knuckles against the man's chest. "Come on. Admit it." He let his fingers subside to the mattress but not before noting the crinkly texture of Arthur's hair.

"Grandfather had…a different combat philosophy."

Bedwyr laughed loudly. "That's understating it."

Arthur turned his head to speak over his shoulder. "He respected Lord Uthyr."

"Everyone respects Lord Uthyr. Unwise not to," he said wryly. As much as his father had ranted at the dinner table about the Roman's methods, though, he wouldn't have let the old soldier continue training young warriors if he hadn't seen value in doing so. And he couldn't remember Uthyr ever crossing Master Wolf. "He respected your grandfathers too, you know."

"No, he didn't."

"He recognized their skills."

"Didn't think much of their partnership."

He couldn't deny that. As a boy, he'd heard enough slurs about what might occur in Marcus Roman's bedchamber that he'd done everything he could to ignore his own body's urges. Training for battle had been a much safer course. "I don't think he understood it."

"They survived the fall of Rome with it," Arthur said, defensive. "Rebuilt a life."

"I know." The Romans had left these islands long before Bedwyr's grandfather had been born. He tried to imagine what the aftermath might have looked like. According to Master Philip, it had caused chaos in Gaul.

Arthur was quiet for a long moment, though not still. His body felt rigid. "What did…what did you think of it?"

"Of what?"

"Their partnership."

"I respected it."

"Oh." He sounded disappointed, and Bedwyr wondered if he could sense it hadn't been the entire truth, which was that the bond between the two men had been revelatory. They had seemed the stronger for it, and their devotion to each other, though subdued, had been evident enough that Bedwyr had had to turn his eyes from it sometimes, lest he give away his own hunger.

He stared at the fire burning low in the hearth, and the words came before he could decide whether they were wise. "I wanted something like it myself."

"You wanted a wife?"

A flame rose from the glowing log in the grate to lick at the air. "Not a wife."

Now Arthur *was* still—almost strangely so, as if he'd suddenly become aware he was naked and pressed up against another man just as naked.

Bedwyr waited, feeling every point of contact between their bodies.

Arthur cleared his throat. "Me neither."

The lightning bolt was back, and crackling.

Bedwyr leaned in to it, destruction be damned.

CHAPTER 10

He set his hand flat against Arthur's chest and felt his heart thump inside the hard cage of his ribs. The pulse of it showed in Arthur's neck. Bedwyr touched his lips to it and smoothed his palm upward. Arthur inhaled deeply, then held it in, his body rigid once more.

Bedwyr raised his forearm, pressing Arthur's head back, and spoke into his ear. "Breathe, cub."

The trapped air gusted out of him, and Bedwyr's hand ate up the contractions of the lean muscle under it. Sliding sideways, he brushed his fingers over Arthur's nipple.

"Gods."

He sounded choked, so different from his usual voice that Bedwyr wanted to hear it again. "Yes?"

"Yes."

Scarcely a whisper. That wouldn't do. He pinched.

Arthur gasped loudly and his whole body arched, pressing his head into Bedwyr's shoulder, his arse up Bedwyr's thigh. He found the other nipple and squeezed it slowly until one of Arthur's hands slapped back to grip Bedwyr's hip. His cock was already well awake and paying attention, but at the hard clutch of Arthur's fingers, it grew heavy.

He eased his hand down Arthur's front, giving him plenty of time to push him away or change his course.

He didn't.

His fingers scraped past Arthur's navel, his belly there tight on strained breaths. When his knuckles bumped into a hard cock, he stopped, brushing them lightly over the hot skin.

How long had he wanted something like this? Now that he lay skin to skin with another, he wondered if he would do it right. As many times as he'd imagined some scenario like this, he hadn't accounted for the other man's weight or strength. As in dreams, the men in the encounters he'd imagined—though sometimes recognizable—had been physically insubstantial. Seldom had he been able to touch them and feel supple flesh or hard bone. They hadn't wriggled against him or had hair on their arses that brushed his legs. They hadn't had bony ankles that scraped his own, hadn't gulped air as if there weren't enough of the stuff in the chamber. They hadn't smelled of their day's work so that he'd wanted to bathe them with his tongue.

None of those apparitions had been real. Any warrior knew he could only envision a fight so far. At some point, he had to armor up and face a man whose object was to kill him.

Secretly, though, Bedwyr was glad Arthur couldn't see him. He brushed his mouth up the cub's neck. "What do you want? Show me."

The hand gripping his hip let go and covered his own. Arthur mashed their hands down his cock before guiding Bedwyr to curl his fingers around it. He squeezed Bedwyr's hand once, then gripped the edge of the mattress.

He'd seen Arthur's cock, of course. He'd seen the cock of every man in the village at some point. At rest, Arthur's was unremarkable, except that it lay in a nest of fiery hair. Now, lying behind him and unable to see either, Bedwyr closed his eyes and imagined.

The cock was longer than his grip, somewhat lanky, like Arthur himself. His fingers surrounded it fully; Arthur wasn't as thick as Bedwyr was. He was no boy either, though, so perhaps it was time to stop thinking of him as a lad. He'd always been Cai's younger brother, mouthy and annoying, more talk than good sense. Someone who needed protecting from himself. But the person arching against Bedwyr now, writhing to encourage him to stroke, was a man, with a man's wants and a man's voice.

"Fuck."

A man's orders.

He stroked his full length, and Arthur shuddered. After a few pulls, Bedwyr slid his hand down over the sac beneath. Arthur lifted his leg to let him in. Curling his fingers around the man's stones, he pressed into the flesh behind them.

Arthur groaned and grabbed the bed frame.

Transfixed by the desperate clutch of Arthur's hands, Bedwyr took hold of his cock again and began to stroke in earnest. Arthur's legs straightened as he shoved his prick into Bedwyr's fist. It pushed and pulled, growing harder as Arthur thrust. Bedwyr chased him with his own hips, pressing his throbbing cock into the tight muscle at the small of Arthur's back.

Arthur pushed back.

It was awkward. As much as he'd been using his left hand in recent weeks, he'd not done this even for himself yet. But who was he to claim any finesse to begin with? He'd only ever been pleasured by his father's women, and he'd kept the encounters as brief as possible, just enough to keep Uthyr from suspecting his true want. He'd never played the lover, never really reciprocated. He'd begun to think he'd only ever be able to do so in his imagination.

If the whispers he'd caught from the women around the village were true, and the prospects on the male side of things as lacking as they'd always seemed, Arthur hadn't been with anyone at all.

Some possessive instinct made him want to be the first, to own this memory in Arthur's mind. He squeezed his cock. "You want more?"

"*Yes.*"

Growled. That was more like it. "How? Tell me."

"Faster. Just...faster." He half shouted when Bedwyr complied.

"Yeah?"

"Yeah."

He stroked hard, his fist bumping the tight sac guarding Arthur's stones. "How long?"

"Long as it takes."

Cheeky. "No," he chuckled, panting. "How long have you wanted it?" He'd wanted to fuck someone with a prick since his pubic hair had come in, so—

"Since your first patrol."

His hand stuttered to a halt. His first... "What?"

Arthur gripped his hand. "Don't stop."

Bedwyr rose on an elbow so he could see Arthur's face. "You've wanted this?"

Arthur's eyes were wide and staring but not at him.

"Look at me."

He did, and the force of it pushed air from Bedwyr's lungs. Arthur swallowed hard. "Please."

The possessiveness in him twisted itself into something more familiar, and he surrounded the cub with the shelter of his body. He resumed his stroking. "Like this?"

"Yes."

He did his best, distracted as he was by the contortions of Arthur's face. How his brows were drawn as if he were in agony. The way his mouth lay open against the mattress, the jerking of his hips as he fucked Bedwyr's fist. Something grew in his chest at the notion that he was the one causing this, and that something felt like responsibility. What little experience he'd had must be brought to bear, to make this right and good.

He also felt a fierce pride in Arthur. He had faced Bedwyr and asked for what he wanted, and now was taking it. He'd strapped on his armor and faced his opponent, except Bedwyr didn't want to end him. He wanted to give him everything.

"Ah—" Arthur stretched against him. His eyes closed before flashing open again. "It's happening."

"What is?"

"Fuck," he moaned. "*Fuck.*"

Arthur's body seized, and seed shot from his cock. It pulsed in Bedwyr's fist as it spent itself. He milked it until the curve of Arthur's arse pressed against the underside of Bedwyr's prick. Letting go of the man, he gripped himself as best he could between their bodies and stroked. The firelight etched sharp shadows along Arthur's ribs and shone on their ridges as he breathed. This was life, this man and the fire that shaped him in the dark for Bedwyr to see. He wanted it, clutched and pulled desperately to be part of it, and then he was spattering Arthur's back with slick streaks.

He stared at them, panting, as they began to drip down his skin. When they touched the bedding, he pushed on Arthur's shoulder until he lay on his back.

"What did you mean, since my first patrol?"

The light was dim, but still he could see the wariness in Arthur's eyes when they met his. Part of him wanted to temper whatever made Arthur look that way. But the warrior he'd been made into knew to strike when the other man was most vulnerable.

He didn't expect to get struck in return.

"That's when I started wanting you," Arthur said.

Bedwyr had been…fourteen on that patrol? Hadn't known what to do with wanting men, had subverted his hunger with training, only to find himself surrounded daily and then nightly by everything that tempted him. He'd tried to extinguish it like a lamp wick, and when that didn't work, tried to ignore it. Arthur would have been ten, not even old enough to begin true training.

Arthur looked away, his eyes darting around the dark space. "Papa Wolf saw it first. That's why I went to talk to him this morning. He knew, and he understood. He accepted me."

Envy poked at Bedwyr's gut, digging in with a claw. His own grandfather had died long ago, wasted and bitter, with no care for anyone but himself. And his father… How would his life have been different if Uthyr had seen this in him? Had pulled him aside one day and told him he wasn't somehow broken?

Arthur let out a shaky breath. "And he knew you were the source."

The envy grew a tendril of hope. "Did he see it in me?"

"No."

He'd worked hard to hide it. So why should he now feel disappointment that he hadn't betrayed himself?

"He warned me not to get my hopes up, that what he'd found with Grandfather had been sheer luck. But you know me." He chuckled ruefully. "I don't listen."

"Good."

Arthur turned back to him.

"Only you know who you truly are. Don't give that up for anyone."

"He was a good man."

"He was. But he and Master Marcus…what they had wasn't luck. They worked for it."

"I know." Arthur cocked his chin as if pleased Bedwyr recognized that. "He only meant he was lucky Grandfather was inclined to be that sort of partner. They were easy with each other, but I'd heard enough stories from my parents and Master Philip to know it was as much a part of their work as forging blades or training men to defend themselves." He smiled sheepishly. "Figured I could work at least as hard as they had. If they hadn't given up, why should I?"

"Stubborn arse."

Arthur blinked.

"Stubborn when Cai knocked you down. Stubborn in the training yard." He gritted his teeth. "Stubborn with Saxons at your throat."

Arthur's smile slipped.

Bedwyr shifted closer. "Then you brought yourself up here. Camped outside in the sleet until I let you in. Built a fire I didn't need. Dogged me 'til I lifted my sword, then ate half my food."

"I—"

Bedwyr stopped him with a warning finger to the lips. "You push me when I'm tired. Pull me when I'm frustrated. Gather firewood, haul water, and catch fish. And to cap it, every night, by that fire you insist on, you strip to your skin so that I have no choice but to see you, every fucking inch." He pressed on Arthur's lower lip, feeling its plump give. "You're stubborn, cub. And gods help me, I like you that way."

When Arthur's eyes widened in surprise, Bedwyr kissed him.

At first he could only sense pressure, the hard shapes of Arthur's teeth behind his lips. Then a suck of air from the man reminded him to breathe, and he tasted it: a flavor like apples, as sweet and tart as the cider brewed after the autumn harvest.

He hated cider. But this…

This he liked.

When he dipped his tongue for more, Arthur gave his own in return. It was a wet, sloppy exchange, and Bedwyr nearly laughed at the thought that they'd both killed men but neither of them had kissed anyone before. He hadn't, anyway, and now found himself lapping greedily at Arthur as if to make up for all the imagined others. Arthur seemed just as eager, his fingers sliding into Bedwyr's hair and clutching, sending a shiver across his scalp. It traveled down his spine and limbs, almost like the battle-fire he felt mid-skirmish.

But he didn't know how to direct this fire, and it felt dangerous. Weapon or tool, it felt just as gods-gifted as the battle-flame, and just as irreversible should he wield it carelessly. He pulled away. Settled on his side again. Willed his breath to slow.

Arthur watched him, his mouth glistening in the firelight.

Bedwyr cleared his throat. "So."

"So."

He reached for something to say. "We should use the shields soon."

Arthur's eyebrows rose. "Tomorrow morning?"

"No."

A grin at his reluctance, then Arthur's expression grew more guarded, his eyes like storm clouds in the dim light. "And tomorrow night?"

Who were they fooling? No one in this hut or this bed. "It's bound to be cold."

Arthur nodded solemnly. "Winter usually is."

Bedwyr chuckled.

The bunk creaked as Arthur rolled over and backed into his chest. "Goodnight, Bedwyr."

His long, warm body invited Bedwyr to draw him in closer. The glow from the hearth played on his hair. Bedwyr nuzzled it, storing the scent in his memory, then yawned. "Fire bright, cub."

A strong hand covered his and squeezed, and a good day became a dreamless night.

CHAPTER 11

When Bedwyr woke to find Arthur still in his bed, he decided it was going to be another good day.

His stump tingled, his arm having played pillow to Arthur's head all night. Carefully, he eased out from under him. Arthur sighed and rolled onto his back, his rangy shoulders moving into the space Bedwyr had just vacated to shift his arm. It gave him an opportunity to study the man who had moved against him hours before.

He was a grown man, if only just. Even in the hazy light of dawn he could see the strong bones of Arthur's face that had displaced the relative softness of boyhood. His skin was winter-pale and freckled. Strong, straight eyebrows gave him an expressive face when he was awake. In sleep, they made him look more serious, leading the eye to the long, hard ridge of his nose. His lips rested slack, just enough to see the edges of his teeth. A fine, pale scar bisected the bottom lip, and Bedwyr vaguely recalled Cai busting it during a tussle. Or three.

Arthur's beard was a darker red than his other hair and hadn't filled in as much as it might later. Letting his eyes wander downward, Bedwyr spotted the pulse that beat in the man's throat and in the hollow between his collar bones. He followed one ridge of bone to Arthur's shoulder and the dark blue figure on his upper arm.

Arthur had had it forever, it seemed—a tattoo badly done because in a moment of poor judgment he'd given it to himself. Bedwyr still remembered the gathering of the village in the meeting hall when Arthur had apologized for stealing Dafydd's ink and needle. He'd insulted their people's tradition, claiming ink before he'd earned it as a warrior. Cai had been especially incensed, since he and Bedwyr had just earned their own first tattoos. Their people had lived in relative peace then, so he and Cai hadn't seen a fight, had only to complete their first patrol to get inked. Evidently even that had been enough for Arthur to covet. As punishment, Uthyr had demanded Arthur apologize to their entire village. Bedwyr had felt pride in his own tattoo and shared some of Cai's sense of injustice. All the same, he'd felt for Arthur as the skinny lad stood alone before their neighbors to face their disapproval.

He wasn't so skinny anymore. With a cautious hand, Bedwyr lifted the blankets away, revealing Arthur's chest and belly. The lines of his body were flatter here than Bedwyr's, and all of them drew his attention downward. He wanted to shove his fingers into the thatch of hair around Arthur's prick. The cock itself rested in the crease of his groin. His stones hung one above the other in a sac Bedwyr wanted to lick. He settled for grazing a thumb across Arthur's thigh.

Arthur blinked awake. His quick eyes took in the hut, the state of the blankets, and Bedwyr's roving hand. As Arthur began to focus on him, Bedwyr realized he hadn't thought this far ahead. He pulled his hand away.

His bedmate shifted onto his side to face him. Bedwyr leaned back minutely, but it was enough to push his back into the wall.

Arthur seemed to realize he'd trapped him. He gave a cocky grin.

Damn it.

Arthur shifted even closer, if that was possible, and set a hand to Bedwyr's ribs. "Had to leave early yesterday. No need today."

Oh, there was plenty of need today on Bedwyr's quarter of the mattress.

But now that Arthur was watching him, he didn't know how to begin. Seeking a distraction from the intensity of Arthur's gaze, touched the old tattoo with a fingertip. "What is this, anyway?"

Arthur huffed a short laugh, as if he knew what Bedwyr was about, and without warning wrapped his fingers around Bedwyr's cock. He squeezed. "Suppose I should return the favor." Arthur stroked up his length. "Like that?"

Not really. Arthur was gripping him too tightly.

Bedwyr took hold of his wrist and pulled his hand away. Rising onto his knees, he caged him, pinning Arthur's hand over his head. Arthur watched him, mouth open slightly as when he'd been sleeping, except that now his breaths came more quickly. Gone was the cocky cub. Now Arthur seemed interested only in what Bedwyr would do next.

He wondered himself. Below him lay a stretch of male flesh he'd never thought to see from this angle. Moreover, it was long, warm, and willing, and Bedwyr found himself extraordinarily hungry for a taste of it.

He began near Arthur's wrist. Tracking a vein that pulsed blue along his forearm, Bedwyr licked to the cub's elbow, then up his biceps. The muscle tensed under his mouth, and he gave it a light bite.

A short, sharp exhale sounded near his ear. "Gods."

Following the contour of shoulder, he brushed his way down Arthur's chest. His ribs rose and fell rapidly, seeming to offer his nipples for Bedwyr's taking. So he did.

Arthur's morning-rough voice filled the hut as Bedwyr swiped one of the small knots with his tongue. Arthur's free hand gripped the back of Bedwyr's neck. Using his short arm, he pressed Arthur's wayward one back onto the mattress. Arthur arched under him, as if he couldn't get close enough. Bedwyr took a nipple and sucked.

Arthur groaned.

He tried to keep the pressure light, but Arthur kept pushing up into him. Reversing course, he sucked harder. Arthur responded immediately, his voice and body pushing for more. Bedwyr gave it to him until he was certain the cub would flinch away. But he didn't, and so Bedwyr licked across his chest and gave the other nipple a thorough lashing.

When he raised his head again, Arthur lay gasping, eyes wide. The sight made Bedwyr feel...

Powerful.

He snagged Arthur's gaze, then lowered his head again. This time, he let the hair on the cub's chest and belly tickle his nose as he worked southward. Arthur's navel was a bump like his nipples. Flicking it with his tongue did make Arthur flinch. His scent grew stronger as Bedwyr edged backward on the mattress, until he came to that coppery nest of hair and the parts of Arthur he'd not been able to see the night before.

His prick was blood-hard now and as erect as a gods-stone. At its base lay something far more tempting than the flowers Bedwyr had seen at the few standing stones he'd encountered. The cub's sac was rosy and not quite drawn tight yet so that he could see the shapes inside. Lowering his mouth, he used his tongue to trace the curve of one.

Arthur's legs fell open.

As Bedwyr glanced up at him, the cub laid a hand on his cock, pressing it to his belly. Out of Bedwyr's way, he guessed. Playfully, he knocked Arthur's hand away and smiled when it gripped the bedding instead. Then he buried his face in the man's musky heat.

The pesky hand landed on his head again, but this time he didn't remove it. Letting it tell him what Arthur—increasingly incoherent—couldn't articulate, he took first one stone into his mouth, sucking lavishly, then the other. Arthur's feet, spread wide, pushed at the blankets, scraped the wall and bed frame. One heel hit the floor before Bedwyr slipped his arms under Arthur's legs and held them to the sides of his neck. Still Arthur writhed and pushed, but it only served to mash himself against Bedwyr's face, into his mouth and nose. When Arthur had begun to cough on the effort to breathe, Bedwyr rose onto his elbows and took Arthur's cock into his mouth.

Arthur grew still, so still Bedwyr looked up to make sure he hadn't stopped breathing altogether.

He hadn't. He was only watching now, with more intensity than Bedwyr had seen in his eyes outside of the training yard. Holding those eyes, he sucked toward the tip of Arthur's cock.

Arthur inhaled sharply and swallowed. His mouth moved as though he wanted to say something—maybe was saying something—but Bedwyr didn't need words. The man's body spoke plainly enough. Closing his eyes, he spread his hand on Arthur's belly, felt and listened and took in his scent, and took him down again.

It was easier than he'd ever imagined, and he had imagined this many, many times. About Arthur since he'd come to the hut. About Master Matthias several times. About Tiro once or twice after a good sparring session. In the dark, curtained space of his bed at home, he had used his fingers. When he found it difficult to forget they were of himself, he'd discovered a trick: strangling his wrist until the fingers on that hand grew numb. Afterward, he could stroke them into his mouth for several minutes and imagine they were another man's cock.

Seemed he'd become rather adept; Arthur was all but wild under him now, kicking and thrusting, his long, hard fingers clutching Bedwyr's hair. The best part was the way he choked out Bedwyr's name and *please*. He'd wanted to taste the man, and he was—was getting a meal's worth, by the gods—but the noises Arthur made were what fed him. He could feel himself growing with each one, his muscles filling with strength. The dragon in him was rising to its haunches, spreading its great red wings. All its power was surging through him as he subjugated the man under him, brought him to a gasping surge of his own.

He readied himself, though this was something he hadn't been able to train for, and the first thick spurt made him pull back. He was glad for it after the fact, as it allowed him to taste this part of Arthur too, this part that no one—save maybe for Arthur himself—had ever tasted. It held the same appley tang as the rest of him but with a bitter undertone, like ale. He sucked at it greedily, until Arthur's hands pulled him off.

"Too much," he coughed.

Bedwyr let him go. Of course it was too much—even Eira knew that and eased off at the end. He resolved to become at least as good at this as she was. Cupping Arthur's spent cock, he brushed his mustache up its length, eliciting one last shudder from Arthur. Then he rose and caged him.

Arthur was staring at him, speechless in a way Bedwyr had never witnessed. The cub had been subdued when he'd first arrived, and it had been enough of a change in demeanor that it disoriented Bedwyr. He'd known Arthur most of his life; except for growing from children to adults, their people were as reliably unchangeable as the mountains amid which they lived.

This silence, this stillness, was something else entirely. It wasn't a muting of the younger man's character. This was Arthur at his most aware, all his senses trained on one moment, one man. Bedwyr's skin prickled to know he was that man, for nothing lay between them but heated breath. This close, Arthur's irises were the soft gray of a dove's feathers. But it was a trick of camouflage for eyes so sharp, for it felt as if Arthur could see past Bedwyr's own eyes and straight on into his mind.

Shielding his thoughts, he glanced away. A deep flush colored Arthur's cheeks and chest. His hair, loose since last night, lay tangled around his neck and across the bedding. Bedwyr plucked it away from Arthur's throat and set his lips there. It contracted under him as Arthur gulped air. With lazy swipes, he licked the sweat from the cub's skin, letting it feed the whole-body hunger growing inside him. When resisting it became a fool's mission, he pushed his nose into the warm muscle of Arthur's neck and lowered his hips until his aching cock rested on the man's belly.

He thrust against the sweat-sticky skin there, then dragged himself back, his mouth falling open on the pleasure that spread through his body. Pressing closer, he mashed himself up Arthur's hard belly. Two strong hands gripped his thighs, began to help him push and drag, until his own legs struggled with the effort. Arthur was groaning under him, more sounds to feed him until he couldn't eat up any more of them. Locking his knees, he ground hard and spent himself between them.

He remained still for a long moment, letting his senses take up again. Arthur breathed deeply under him, his hands now resting on Bedwyr's back. His voice rasped in Bedwyr's ear as he cleared his throat. He smelled good enough to eat.

Again.

In the quiet of the hut, a notion dawned on him alongside the daylight—that this place was theirs. Gwen brought her baskets less frequently now that they mostly fed themselves, and for any number of reasons no one else ventured up the path and around the hillside to the shepherd's hut. This small structure with its ramshackle door and aged thatching was theirs for now. This hearth sufficient, and this bed… It creaked and groaned, but it held. At this moment, it held Arthur's vital warmth under him, his own body stretched on top, and the blankets in a tangle around their feet. And they could lie just so for hours if they chose, or they could move against each other until they were too exhausted not to lie just so. Everything they'd just done they could do, in the safety of this place, whenever they wanted it.

He smiled against the pulse ticking in Arthur's throat. He was going to want to do this a lot.

Rising on his elbows, he snared the cub's gaze. "Good morning."

Arthur's face transformed into a grin that lit the dim space around them, and the dark corners inside Bedwyr too. "Can't say I've had a better one."

With that, the sense of power was back. Bedwyr let it guide his fingers into Arthur's long hair, where they curled on a tight hold. Arthur seemed to be waiting, intent on hearing whatever he might say next.

Lowering his head, Bedwyr kissed him hard and deep, content for now to let his body speak for him.

CHAPTER 12

Gods' blood, what had he unleashed?

Arthur didn't know, but as he lay there, pressed into the scratchy ticking by Bedwyr's mass, held in place by him, having his mouth claimed by him, he knew he only wanted to feed whatever beast had awoken in the man above him. Feed it, make it stronger, give it space to grow…and tempt it to use him for all of these things.

What had begun as a forceful, needful kiss was settling into something lazier now. As much as he loved the way Bedwyr kept him just here, and the warm, sticky scrape of his body hair against Arthur's, it also made him impatient. A sense of urgency was welling up in him like water from a spring. He knew the source: Lord Uthyr's command rang in his mind every day here. Recently he'd begun to wonder if he should tell Bedwyr that Uthyr had sent him. Arthur owed him that, surely, after everything Bed had shared of himself. But he couldn't think of a way to convince Bedwyr he would have come anyway since, in fact, he'd needed the push from his warlord.

For now, it would have to remain a secret. But this wellspring of urgency—he needed to capture and drink it while he could.

He broke the kiss. "Ready to get started?"

Bedwyr nipped his lip. "On what?"

"On the day."

Bedwyr nuzzled his neck. "On napping?"

"We just woke up."

The man above him groaned and rolled to the side, but before Arthur could sit up, Bedwyr hooked an arm around his waist and hauled him back into his body. Some more rumbling as Bed settled him against him, then a contented sigh and warm breath on the back of his neck.

"Bed."

No response.

"Bedwyr."

The man's finger tapped Arthur's chin. "Shhh."

"The sun's full up."

"The sun didn't just spend itself."

"What's that to do with it?"

Bedwyr snuffled his hair. "Makes me sleepy."

Arthur rolled to face him. "Spending makes you sleepy?"

"Just said as much." He cracked open one eye to peer at Arthur. "Doesn't it do the same to you?"

Arthur laughed. "No."

A suspicious frown. "What's it do?"

"Stokes the fire. Heats the steel."

The frown became a smirk, and Bedwyr pushed closer. "That's promising."

"It gets the stone rolling downhill. Pushes the fledgling from the nest."

Bed stopped moving. "You lost me."

"It makes me want to attack the day."

"Oh."

"Yeah, so..."

"So..."

Arthur leaned close until their noses touched. "So let's get *up*, man."

"It's cold outside," Bedwyr grumbled. "The bed's warm." He smoothed his hand across Arthur's chest. "You're warm." Thumbed his nipple.

Arthur locked his muscles against the shiver that caused. This was more challenging than he'd expected. He needed some sort of enticement. "I'll make you a wager."

"What kind of wager?"

His mind raced. "Whoever bests the other in sparring today gets a thorough rub-down tonight."

Bed's eyes narrowed. "How thorough?"

"Thorough."

That gaze roved down his body. "How will we determine who's won the spar?"

"Won't need to. I'll win it."

Bedwyr's eyes flashed up to meet his. "You think so, do you?"

The challenge in the question stroked Arthur's stones as fully as the man's hand could have done. As his tongue *had* done. "I do."

Bedwyr looked at him for a few seconds, then gave him a hard shove. Arthur landed on the cold packed-dirt floor with a grunt. Bed's feet swung around to the floor, and he stood. From Arthur's vantage point, he looked massive. Almost as big as his grin.

"Off your lanky arse, cub. Sun's climbing."

Now that was more like it. Arthur stood, rubbing the ache in his rump with a scowl to mask the triumph he felt at getting Bedwyr moving. As they threw on their clothes and grabbed bites to eat, his mind raced ahead to create a challenge for the day that would meet that balance he wanted to achieve. As much as he might have liked to have the soreness of training pushed from his muscles, Arthur fully intended to lose the day's practice. The trick would be not letting on he was throwing the match. There'd be blood to pay if Bedwyr sensed that.

By the time they picked up their swords, Arthur had a plan. It began when Bedwyr walked confidently to their trampled training area only to turn and discover Arthur walking away.

"What?" Bedwyr called. "You're giving up already?"

Arthur turned, strolling backward casually. "Too easy."

Bedwyr stuck his sword tip in the ground. "Too easy?"

A hint of warning in his voice, but also a good challenge. Arthur shrugged. "Level ground is nice. Saxons love it."

The other man jerked his sword out of the earth.

Arthur spread his arms to the hills surroundings them. "We Cymry are of the mountains. We don't need a lowlander's safe little patch of flat dirt."

It was something to behold, the fire those words stoked in Bedwyr. Slowly, he turned square to Arthur, his big hand flexing to refine its grip on his blade. Rolling his shoulders, he bared his teeth. A chuckle grated from between them.

Then Bedwyr charged, and the chase was on.

The terrain gave way to slope quickly, giving Arthur just the sort of challenge he was looking for. The snow cover added its own hazards, hiding rocks and holes that caught their boots, forcing them to right themselves or be caught out. Even keeping himself downhill, though, didn't always put Arthur at a disadvantage versus Bedwyr, as he had several inches on the man. He didn't want to play that scheme all morning anyway, or Bedwyr would see his game. So, taking full advantage of his longer legs, he skirted Bed to put himself on the same level of the hillside's traverse, then above him for several exchanges of blows.

Soon, though, he was no longer directing the fight alone. Something about the new circumstances was bringing out a fierceness in Bedwyr, as if his body had found its center—its power—on the very unevenness of ground that should have unsettled him.

And that was only right, Arthur thought. These hills had brought Bedwyr into the world, had protected him and trained him right up to manhood and beyond. Of course he was most himself on their steep slopes.

Didn't mean Arthur couldn't use them against him. Checking that the slope behind Bedwyr was relatively clear of obstacles, he stuck a foot behind Bed's and tripped him.

Bedwyr's eyes widened as he felt his balance abandon him, but true to the warrior he was—that Arthur knew still dwelt within the man—he didn't let himself go down alone. Hooking his short arm around Arthur's neck, he toppled him too.

They landed hard on the snowy slope and rolled. Arthur pushed off, and fought to gain his feet first. In this Bedwyr truly did have the upper hand, though, being closer to the earth in general. Arthur was still kneeling when Bedwyr brought his next strike. It had no force behind it, was maybe only a warning, but Arthur wasn't going to find out. They weren't finished—he wasn't finished. Pushing to his full height, he gave Bedwyr his best, driving his boots backward across the face of the hill several paces until Bed caught on to the rhythm. Arthur switched it up then, just enough to keep Bed on his toes, so to speak, and parried until he found his footing again. The third time Arthur would have redirected the spar, however, Bedwyr seized control.

Which was to say, he lowered one shoulder and, tossing his sword aside, drove his body into Arthur's.

The force of it knocked Arthur off his feet. He hit the ground with a grunt and then another as Bedwyr landed on top of him. Letting go his sword, Arthur turned all his limbs to the grapple Bedwyr seemed intent upon having. To anyone watching, they might have seemed to be at each other's throats, so violent was their tussling slide down the hillside.

Up close it was another sort of thing altogether. Yes, Bedwyr was using every fiber of strength he possessed to subjugate Arthur, and yes, Arthur was resisting with every quick move he'd ever attempted in a wrestling match and some he hadn't. But men bent on destroying each other didn't usually laugh while doing so, or make threats of the same variety Bedwyr was dealing him.

"...show you a safe patch of dirt...bunk's not going to be safe...not for you..."

The world spun wildly as they rolled down its plane, snow filling Arthur's mouth and eyes. Blinking hard, he fought to regain some sense of orientation but here as on the battlefield, Bedwyr was singularly focused on the man he fought. Arthur's body felt at once fired to fight the arms and legs binding him, yet tempted to let them wrest his control from him. When the hill dumped them unceremoniously at its base, Arthur gave in to a few seconds of surrender.

Straddling his body, his hair and beard crusted with snow, Bedwyr looked like a vengeful ice god come to earth to wreak havoc on unsuspecting mortals. He'd pinned Arthur's arms with his own. His boots were hooked over Arthur's splayed knees. When he said, "Give?" Arthur thought he might give anything the man asked for.

But what fun would that be?

"Never," he said and surged up, tipping Bedwyr sideways. Scrambling to his feet, he flung snow at him. Bed spat and roared, and Arthur choked on laughter that squeezed his lungs like a bellows. Shouting hoarsely, he ran for the stream ahead. It was the same rill that ran behind the shepherd's hut. Its own tumble down the hillside was gentler than theirs had been, but its crystalline tinkling promised a chilly comeuppance for the second man to reach it.

"Don't do it, cub, unless you want a bath!"

Grinning, Arthur led the chase. Gaining the stream first, he splashed into it, scarcely aware of the cold water as it seeped through the seams of his boots, so intent was he on the man running at him. As Bedwyr's first boot splashed down, Arthur feinted left and sent a two-handed scoop of icy water into his pursuer's face.

Bedwyr sputtered and bent to send up his own sling of water. It caught Arthur on the neck, slipping chilly fingers down his chest and belly. Bending, he sent up another spray, and for several seconds they might have been boys who'd found an opportunity to shirk their chores in favor of a swim, never mind it was the dead of winter and no fool, not even a lad of nine, would wade in and still claim a sound mind.

But they were well past believing they had their heads about them, and now there was nothing for it but that one of them best the other, wet clothes and frozen beards be damned. Arthur splashed once more, buying himself a second or two to contrive his next move, but it was a second or two too many and then Bedwyr had hold of his shirt.

Arthur grappled with him, thinking he might trip him again. But the slick stones of the creek bed betrayed him and his boot slipped. He flailed to keep his balance, but by then Bedwyr had overbalanced too, and they went down with a cold splash that sucked the air from Arthur's lungs. The flow of the stream, so mild at the top of the hill, was more substantial here and soaked him to the skin in an instant. He shuddered against it, shouting.

Bedwyr was just as wet but, sitting astride Arthur, he seemed completely unaffected, damn him.

"Give."

"No."

Bedwyr leaned down, his grin becoming a snarl. "Give."

His face was inches from Arthur's. His eyes seemed to dance with the tumble of the water. "Make me," Arthur said. Because he could. He would.

Bedwyr grunted and pressed into him, grinding his hips hard into Arthur's. "Give, cub."

The retort was on his lips, but then a fresh flow of icy water made his entire body seize. He fought against it, but shaking overtook his body and he stopped struggling. "I give."

Bedwyr pulled back. "I win?"

"You win!" Arthur gasped.

Bedwyr smiled. In the next moment, he was pulling Arthur to his feet. With an arm around his middle, Bedwyr helped him out of the stream.

As he stood on the bank, water dripping from every part of him, Arthur scanned the scuffed hillside. "Where are our swords?"

"I'll fetch them," Bedwyr said. "You get up to the hut and the fire." He slapped Arthur on the arse. "Go."

CHAPTER 13

Arthur climbed the hill, his legs burning by the time he neared the hut. He looked behind him once, to where Bed was kicking through the snow for their blades.

"I said go!" came the warning call.

The inside of the hut was marginally warmer than the air outdoors. Crossing to the hearth, he knelt and blew on the coals to revive them. Feeding the small flames fuel, he had a decent fire built when the door shifted behind him.

"Why are you still dressed?"

He rose and turned to Bedwyr, ready to tease him for his aggression but found him scowling.

Bed stomped over to him, leaving snow-edged boot prints on the floor. "Get this off," he said, plucking at Arthur's soaked shirt.

Arthur's fingers felt cramped, but he managed to unfasten his belt and tossed it aside. Peeling his shirt over his head, he flung it over a beam. His boots were stubborn but gave up their hold after some tugging. When it came to the laces on his trousers, he fumbled on purpose.

Bedwyr knocked his hands aside and knelt before him. Frowning with concentration, he worked the wet ties loose, his other arm braced naturally against Arthur's hip. When he could, he peeled the wool down Arthur's legs. When he straightened, he came level with Arthur's hardening cock. It seemed to snag his attention, which only fired Arthur's blood-rush. Mere inches separated Arthur from the wet heat of Bedwyr's mouth. All it would take was for one of them to lean toward the other.

Instead, Bedwyr rose and snatched a blanket off the bunk. He tossed it to Arthur. "Get warm."

Arthur pretended to do so, half-facing the fire, blanket around his shoulders but open to the heat rising from the flames. His attention, though, was all on Bedwyr, who was stripping his own clothes. He did so quietly and efficiently, baring his body in the way only a man bent on warming himself did. Only when Bedwyr peeled his wet trousers from his legs did Arthur realize how nimbly the man's fingers had dispatched the sodden laces singlehanded.

Grabbing a second blanket, Bedwyr wrapped his own shoulders and crossed the small space to stand next to Arthur. Now that they stood side by side, naked but for wool blankets, Arthur couldn't think of a thing to say. Either Bedwyr couldn't either or wasn't inclined to, because the only sounds in the hut were the crackling of the fire and the small *pat-pat-pat* of their queues dripping on the dirt floor. He reached back and squeezed the water from his hair. The splash of it on his ankles made him shiver.

Bedwyr looked over at him, one dark eyebrow raised. "Good day for a swim?"

Arthur groaned. "No need to rub it in."

Bedwyr smiled and turned back to the fire. "I thought the rub was the point."

The full prospect of what lay ahead struck Arthur: his hands on Bedwyr from head to foot and everywhere between. Another shudder racked his body. Bedwyr grunted softly, then draped his blanket around Arthur's shoulders.

"What about you?"

"Let me in," Bedwyr said quietly, then ducked under one of Arthur's arms to stand close behind him. The brush of his hair against Arthur's bare back made his skin flinch. But then Bedwyr's arms came around his middle and pulled him back into his solid warmth. Arthur slumped against him.

"Better?"

"Yes."

Bedwyr's hand came to rest on his belly. After a few breaths that Bedwyr took but Arthur held, the hand pressed into him.

It was as warm as the rest of Bed and heavy with intent. Arthur let it rove up to his chest, across to his ribs, before he interrupted its progress.

"You won the wager. Lie down and I'll rub you."

Bedwyr didn't speak for a moment, and more important, didn't lie down. "I want a different prize."

Disappointment prodded Arthur. His hands wanted their fill of the man behind him. "What makes you think that's up for the taking?"

"I won the wager."

Well, he couldn't argue with that, damn the logic. "What do you want?" His boots oiled, probably.

"I'll rub you."

The hand pressed up his sternum, leaving a trail of heat.

That hand would be all over him. But wouldn't it frustrate Bedwyr not to have his other hand to work with? Would it be a reminder of his limitations?

"Is that a problem?"

Arthur shook his head until he could coordinate his tongue. "No."

"Lie down here."

Arthur spread the blankets before the hearth and lay down. The wool tempered the chill of the floor before it could press into his body. Then he felt Bedwyr straddle his hips and let his weight settle there.

It made Arthur feel caged but when Bed's hand pushed up his spine, he decided he didn't mind. After several such passes, he felt Bed's other arm flat at his lower back before it mashed its way up and over his shoulder blade. He groaned with the release of tension there.

After a while, Bedwyr seemed to sit up and for several seconds his palm smoothed over Arthur's skin. "You've a fine back," he said. "Strong."

The words fed some hungry part of him. "Training, I guess."

Bedwyr grunted agreement, pressing a thumb along Arthur's spine. "More years than most."

Arthur set his forehead to the blanket as a bolt of gratitude shot through him. Wasn't this what he'd always wanted? That Bedwyr would notice him, notice his hard effort?

Still, for all that work, he had no ink. Not only had he not earned it, he'd thrown away his chance at it and harmed Bedwyr in doing so. He couldn't bring himself to say as much. Settled instead for, "More to learn."

That thumb rubbed hard down one side of his spine to his lower back. "Always that, for every man."

Bed's weight eased, and he shifted down to settle above Arthur's knees. The movement exposed more of Arthur's body, and he shivered. Bedwyr seemed to read his mind and spread his hand over one arsecheek. Arthur resisted the urge to push up into Bed's hold. He waited, almost convinced he could feel every ridge of Bedwyr's fingerprints.

"You've a fine arse, too."

The words, delivered in a thoughtful rumble, made him smile. "It's an arse."

Bedwyr snorted.

"What?"

"I'll let that go since you can't see for yourself."

"What's so fine?"

Bedwyr gripped one cheek. "Firm. Lean."

"Cai's got the same."

"Never noticed."

"So's Papa. Mama's always telling us to get our skinny arses to the table—"

Bedwyr slapped Arthur's rump. The sharp smack left a sting that felt as though he'd been branded. A moment later Bedwyr's chest lay against Arthur's back, and his voice was in his ear. "When I pay compliment to your arse, don't bring up your father."

Arthur shut up.

Bedwyr worked his way down Arthur's body at an excruciatingly slow pace. By the time he said "Turn over," Arthur was blood-hard.

Bedwyr watched Arthur's prick as it swayed above his stones like a spear freshly stuck in the earth. Then he began to rub Arthur's feet.

Arthur groaned with frustration.

"You said thorough," Bed said in a tediously calm voice.

"I know what I said."

"Wouldn't want to give your ankles short shrift." His fingers kneaded one such ankle.

Arthur shifted, and his cock wobbled like a drunken man. "Good of you."

"Only fulfilling the wager."

Except that when his hand and arm had pressed up Arthur's thighs, leaving his skin tingling in their wakes, Bedwyr neatly skirted

Arthur's prick.

Arthur stared as Bedwyr focused instead on Arthur's hips, then his chest, then his arms. Through it all, Arthur's cock stood tall, hoping to gain the blasted man's attention, to no avail. When Bedwyr gave him a smack on the shoulder and rose to his feet, Arthur gaped after him.

"Forgetting something?"

Bedwyr turned, eyebrows raised in curiosity. "What?"

Arthur waved toward his prick, which in turn waved at Bedwyr.

Bedwyr tipped his head. "Suppose I missed it." He shrugged. "Next time."

Arthur clambered to his feet and took the pace and a half required to loom over Bedwyr. "The wager was for a thorough rub-down."

Bed met his frown with an unperturbed expression. "Then you shouldn't have thrown the match."

Arthur's mouth was open but with what retort he couldn't have said. He shut it. Opened it again. "I didn't."

"You did."

"Didn't—"

He fell silent as the other man wrapped his meaty hand around Arthur's hard cock.

But Bedwyr didn't move. No pull, no stroke, not even a squeeze. Only a loose hold that nevertheless rooted Arthur to the ground.

Bedwyr gave him a smile. "You'll make it up to me with a trout, fresh from the stream and roasted 'til it's crisp and dripping. Then, this afternoon, we'll spar again." His fingers slid to the base of Arthur's prick and across his tight stones.

Arthur gulped a breath.

Bedwyr leaned close. "If you want me to finish you off—*thoroughly*—you'll fight as if you mean to win."

~

The trout was waiting in the trap, as if in league with Bedwyr.

Arthur paced next to the fire pit as the fish dripped grease into the flames. Then he paced as Bedwyr sat on a stump next to the fire and ate the fish, taking his time and licking his fingers, one by one. When Bedwyr stood and retired to the hut for midday nap, Arthur paced circles around the hut, too restless even to collect firewood.

Finally, when the sun was high, Bedwyr emerged with his sword and Arthur's. "Spar?" he asked in the most offhand sort of way.

Arthur won, decisively.

No cheating, no pulling his strikes. Nor did he humiliate Bedwyr, only brought his best work and depended on Bed to meet it. He did, which made Arthur proud. But not so proud he forgot his own mission.

As soon as Bedwyr conceded, Arthur stalked back to the stream. Not waiting for the other man, he stripped to the skin and stepped into the chilly water for the third time that day.

Bedwyr did the same, splashing handfuls across his chest. "I was thinking of taking a walk," he said as if making small talk.

A walk, eh?

Arsehole.

Arthur rubbed water up the inside of his thigh to give his sac a seemingly thoughtful washing. The cold drew up his stones, but the look on Bedwyr's face was worth the discomfort. "Where to?" he asked, giving his prick a lazy pull and enjoying the way Bed's eyes followed his every move.

They met Arthur's. "Straight into that hut."

"Short walk."

"Work to do."

He could feel Bedwyr stalking him as they carried their clothes back to the hut. Taking any advantage he could conceive, Arthur stretched his arms high as if working out soreness and then reached back to rub one of his arsecheeks.

A very gratifying growl sounded behind him.

Scarcely had the door of the hut been shoved into place than they collided. Hot mouths and cold hands, none of which could get enough of what they sought.

"I was thinking," Arthur said hoarsely, "of a different prize."

Bedwyr grabbed Arthur's hair and sucked at his neck. "You want my mouth on your cock or not?"

Arthur knew when he was bested. "Fuck, yes."

"On the bed."

Arthur lay down on the blankets. Bedwyr knelt next to the bunk.

"Aren't you going to—"

Bedwyr's hand covered his mouth. When Arthur made to speak anyway, Bedwyr pressed hard.

Shocked by the force of it, Arthur stilled, his attention on a blade's edge. Then Bedwyr lowered his head to surround Arthur's prick with wet heat, and his concentration snapped.

It should have felt familiar; Bedwyr had only just done this at dawn. And it did. There was Bed's tongue, and his beard, and *gods*, his teeth. There was his nose pressed hard into Arthur's groin and his hair spread over Arthur's thighs. And there were the noises he made, the sorts of sounds that might come from a starving man at a harvest feast.

All of that was the same, but Bed's hand on his mouth twisted everything into something else. It pinned Arthur to the mattress, commanded his chatter cease. In turn it spoke volumes back to him: that Bedwyr would more than fulfill the wager, that he didn't need even the one hand he still had to do so. That if Arthur would only follow orders and lie back and not talk, Bed would take care of him, finish him off so completely it might kill him.

For that's what it felt like. With one arm and both thighs immobilized, and able to draw breath only through his nose, Arthur closed his eyes, gripped the bedding, and gave in to the pleasure at his center. Slowly, his mind emptied of all but the sounds Bedwyr made and the sensation that he was drawing every sweet thing in the world into his mouth through Arthur's cock. The sweetness grew and grew until it threatened to obliterate everything else, and then it did.

When next he became aware of himself, Arthur was panting. Bedwyr's hand rested on his mouth but lightly. Before he could rub his lips on it, kiss it in thanks, Bedwyr took it back. Rising from his crouch, he stood over Arthur. When Arthur reached for him, Bedwyr shook his head. "Stretch. Arms above your head."

Arthur raised his arms just so, stretching his body as he might after a sparring session, as he had done between the stream and the hut. Bed's eyes seemed to darken as Arthur pulled himself long and tight. Bedwyr's prick stood out straight from his body as if straining toward Arthur's. Bedwyr took himself in hand and after few quick strokes, spent himself on Arthur's hip.

Only then did Bedwyr join him on the creaky bunk, pulling Arthur back into his body. He drew a deep breath before nuzzling Arthur's ear. "Shields tomorrow."

The words made no sense until he spotted Bedwyr's battle shield and his own, propped against the opposite wall where they'd rested for weeks. "All right."

With an agreeable mumble, Bedwyr kissed his neck and then fell to sleep.

Arthur lay awake as Bedwyr dozed and tried to sort in his mind a day that hadn't gone as he'd planned. He was sated, that much he couldn't deny. In fact, he wasn't certain he'd be able to stand if called on to do so any time soon, let alone do the few chores he did here. If he could have, he would lie here with Bed for the rest of the day and on into the night, feeling the man's ribs rise and fall on his breaths and the heavy surety of his arm over Arthur's middle.

But something poked at his mind, some half thought seeking its remainder. For all the day had given him, he was unsatisfied somehow. Closing his eyes, he tried to imagine it, whatever it was he wanted, until it began to come to him in teasing glints, like sun off a fish's scales. Bedwyr's face, his chest. Arthur reaching for him, feeling his skin under his palms, the solid mass of his body in Arthur's hands as Bedwyr moved against him.

He wanted to touch Bedwyr—that was it. Yet spent though he was, his hands felt empty. Thinking back over the times they'd come together like this, a pattern began to show itself, of Bedwyr pulling Arthur's hands away, pinning them to the mattress, ordering them over his head.

Ordering them, in truth. Arthur thought of the power he'd sensed emerge from Bedwyr over the past couple of days, and an unwelcome notion presented itself, that Bedwyr might be lording himself over Arthur as fully as Uthyr had done to send him here—as Uthyr had done for years, insisting he train more, that he wasn't ready for battle.

Had Bed regained so much confidence that he felt he was the warlord's son again? If so, Arthur should be glad for it; hadn't that been his aim these past weeks?

And yet, he didn't think Bedwyr would use him in that way, in the same way he'd admitted to using Eira.

Arthur dismissed the thought before it could sour his stomach. No, Bed had shown himself here, to Arthur—no other.

But for some reason, he wasn't yet showing his full self.

Arthur rose and dressed and went about his chores. Later, as he and Bed passed the evening before the hearth, Arthur's mind turned several paces ahead to a moment when he might catch Bedwyr without his usual defenses.

Settling again for the night, tucked back into Bedwyr's warmth, Arthur decided his moment would be the sleepy stillness just before dawn.

CHAPTER 14

When Bedwyr opened his eyes, Arthur was smiling at him.

Drowsy, he smiled back. He could get used to waking this way.

"Sleep well?"

He yawned, his jaw cracking, and nodded. "You?"

"No."

"Why not?"

"Restless."

Bedwyr stretched. "Wonder what we could do about that."

He didn't hear the mischief in Arthur's chuckle until it was too late.

By that time, Arthur's fingers were digging into his ribs. Bedwyr jerked his arms to his sides to protect himself, but the cub was alarmingly quick, jumping to Bedwyr's belly, his rump, the back of his knee. When one hand prodded his armpit, he shouted. No justice that he had half the hands Arthur had with which to repay the tickling gropes. In fact, Arthur seemed to have sprouted more hands than were his due. He had Bedwyr solidly on the defensive, fending off his clawing fingers and unable to put his own to use.

Then Arthur had him 'round the prick, and they both stilled.

The tussle had made him hard. Arthur's big hand gave him a tight squeeze.

"Not ticklish here, eh?"

Evidently Arthur took his hard swallow, and the silence that followed, as confirmation, for he stroked, his fist like an iron cuff. Bedwyr stared at the man's chest, at the lean muscles moving under his skin. He focused on one rosy nipple. Tried to imagine it in his mouth, how he would suck on it, what sounds that would draw from Arthur.

Arthur shoved his face into Bedwyr's throat, startling him. Everything about him was hard—nose, chin, teeth. His lips. How could lips feel like leather armor?

He let Arthur grind his face into his neck, to nip him unknowingly. He *could* know. Bedwyr could tell him—should tell him—to lighten his touch. He opened his mouth…but he couldn't make himself do it. With a desperate hand, Bedwyr reached for Arthur's hair. Burying his fingers in the long fall of it, he stared at the candle on the table across the hut and tried to quash the panic beginning to bloom in his ribcage.

A knock on the door nearly jolted him out of his skin.

Arthur jerked back, but Bedwyr was already scrambling over him. Grabbing two of the blankets, he stripped them from their nest and threw them on the floor before the hearth.

The knock sounded again. Then, "Bed?"

Cai.

Arthur sat up, but Bedwyr stopped him with a hand on his shoulder. Shaking his head, he pointed to the blankets on the floor, then to himself. Arthur hastily covered himself with the remaining bedding. His lips looked reddened, most likely from Bedwyr's beard. He hoped Cai wouldn't notice.

Thanking the gods that his cock had been shocked into limpness, Bedwyr crossed to the door, grumbling, "Yeah, yeah."

Cai frowned at his nakedness when he shifted the door aside. "Still sleeping?"

"It's scarcely dawn."

"And?" Cai looked into the hut, spotted Arthur on the bed. His eyes immediately roved the space, catching on the mess of blankets before the hearth. He scowled at Arthur. "You took his bed?"

"No."

"You're in it."

"I didn't want it," Bedwyr said, hoping to forestall a guilty blush that might give Arthur away. He grabbed his shirt and drew it over his head. "Why are you pounding on my door at the arsecrack of day?"

"Gwen said you've been training." Cai stepped inside. He picked up an apple from the table and bit into it.

"Did she."

"I might have tickled it out of her."

Images of wrestling with Arthur, of digging his fingers in, this time reducing the cub to gasping surrender. Then images of Cai doing the same to Gwen. His fingernails bit his palm. "You tickled Gwen and got away with your fingers intact?"

Cai held up his left hand, the smallest finger of which had been splinted.

"Serves you right," Bedwyr growled. "Don't touch my sister."

"Didn't mean anything. She's a child."

Arthur snorted. "Bested you."

Cai scowled at him, then shrugged at Bedwyr. "I was up. Just thought I'd come ask. You really fighting with your left hand? That's what Gwen said."

"I am."

"Rough going?"

For all Cai's bluntness, his eyes held genuine understanding. They'd trained together since boyhood. They'd been friends just as long, until his injury. Bedwyr relented. "Not easy. Your brother beats me up daily."

Cai's mouth twisted, and he glared at Arthur. "Ease up."

Arthur swung his legs out of bed and stood, reaching for his shirt where it hung over a rafter. "He's a grown man. He can take what I serve up."

Bedwyr felt his face flush and hoped Cai wouldn't hear any double meaning in his brother's words. "It's been helpful. I need to be able to defend myself."

Cai looked back at him, and it was there in his expression: no more patrols, no more campaigns. Bedwyr was just a villager now, with the bare amount of skill to defend his hearth. It was one thing to say it himself, but to see confirmation in Cai's demeanor, to see pity there...

Cai turned to glance back over his shoulder, shifting on his feet.

Couldn't wait to be gone. It cut deeper than Bedwyr had been prepared for. He looked away. "You'll be wanted in the training yard soon."

Nothing for a moment, then, "All right. I just wanted to see how it was going."

"Thanks."

By the time Cai had rounded the hill back to the village, Arthur was dressed. He came to stand behind Bedwyr and set a warm hand on his shoulder. "We really need to mend this fucking door. I'll take care of it. Spar?"

"Yeah."

They started without their shields. Whether Arthur understood that he couldn't face the thing yet, or just didn't want to force the issue, he said nothing about it. After an hour or so, however, Bedwyr couldn't avoid it any longer. He gave Arthur a resigned nod, and Arthur retrieved the shields from the hut.

Bedwyr's felt awkward, swinging from his forearm because he didn't have a hand to grip the handle and keep the thing upright before his body. The tension he still held in his back and shoulders from Cai's unexpected visit wasn't helping. Why had he proposed using them? Stupid. He called a halt and started to tinker with the straps.

Arthur stepped close to watch. "You need something to stabilize it, eh?"

"It's useless," he snapped. Taking a deep breath, he tried for a more measured tone. "It was kind of your mother to fit these on it…"

"…but it needs something more."

He huffed a frustrated breath from his nose. Arthur set down his sword. Bedwyr thought he would try to help adjust the bindings, but his hand only came to rest on Bedwyr's, stilling it. When he looked up, Arthur was watching him.

"I'll tell her. She'll fix it."

"She doesn't have to—"

"She does. She's the armorer."

Armorers armed men who fought. Not men who played at practice.

"Hey."

He looked at Arthur again.

"She's expecting it. She knew that these"—he indicated the straps—"were only a start. She said so. Besides…" One of his eyebrows rose. "Are you going to tell my mother you don't want her help?"

He shuddered. "Gods, no."

Arthur smiled. "Wise decision. You need to have it done in person, you know. So she can make the adjustments on you, not me."

He'd thought of it, hadn't he, of marching back into the village to prove himself to his father again, to show him just how far he'd come. But when faced with the prospect of walking the path that would take him there…of seeing on others' faces what he'd seen on Cai's… "Never mind. I can get by."

"Get by?"

"It's fine. I'm fine—"

"Bed."

He stopped tugging on the strap and stood still, the name echoing in his scattered mind.

Bed.

Cai called him that; Gwen too. In their voices, it was a friendly, cajoling thing.

In Arthur's it landed more softly, like fingertips in the dark.

He looked from one gray eye to the other, then blinked. "I can't go back."

"Why not?"

"Why do you think?"

"Because he sent you away?"

It would have been easy to agree to that statement. Yes, one didn't ignore one's own banishment. But that wasn't really why he was hesitating.

"Have you considered meeting with him? Showing him what you can do?"

Bedwyr stared at him. Was he that easily read?

Arthur studied his face. "You have, haven't you?" He smiled. "Bed, that's good. You should do it."

"Even if I wanted to, I'm not ready."

Arthur stepped closer. "You are."

"I'm not." Nor for pity, not from Uthyr.

"He would listen," the cub insisted.

"You don't know that!"

Arthur looked away, his jaw working.

Bedwyr was about to call it off, end the discussion—the shield would work, it would be fine—when Arthur gripped his shoulder. It made him flinch.

"Right," Arthur said, not noticing. "No meeting. But you need your shield. The smithy's on the edge of the village. We'll go at night, and I'll bring Mama to you. Nobody else needs to see us. And"—he gave Bedwyr's cheek a light slap—"I'll get what we need to repair the door. All right?"

When had Bedwyr become a man who let fear rule him? He'd always been able to set it down, ignore it and get on with his work. Maybe his work had changed, but he did need his shield, and Arthur seemed confident his mother would help. They would be well away from the meeting hall. And Arthur would be with him. He'd never thought that that would be something he needed, but he did.

It was damned humbling.

He leaned into the man's hold. "All right."

"Yes?"

The laces of Arthur's shirt rose and fell on his breath. Between the cords, the hair on his chest glinted reddish in the early light. Bedwyr stared at it, so different from his own, as if Arthur had been painted by the sun itself. Cai looked more like Master Matthias than Arthur did. So why hadn't he ever felt this pull toward Cai, this nearly unbearable need to touch? It was one thing to give in to it in a night-dark hut; it was something much more exposed to admit in daylight. Even softened by a haze of cloud, the morning light made him feel as though someone had flayed his skin from his body, leaving the deeper flesh bare for everyone to see. For Arthur to see.

Groping in the dark—that he could dismiss as loneliness, isolation, another warm body as frustrated as his own. But if he met Arthur's eyes now, there would be no explaining it away.

One of Arthur's hands rose, his fingers coming to rest under Bedwyr's chin. They pressed upward, and Bedwyr found those dove-colored eyes watching him, looking back and forth between his own. Then Arthur was leaning closer, and closer still, until his lips touched Bedwyr's.

He stood rigid, stupidly clutching his sword, the shield hanging off his right arm.

"Bed," Arthur whispered against him, breath warming his lips. "Kiss me back."

He dropped his sword and wrapped his hand at the back of Arthur's neck.

Arthur groaned.

Bedwyr kissed him.

Outside, by daylight, on their feet. He should have been close to panic again, but he couldn't be bothered to pay it any mind. Arthur tasted sweet and tangy, and at that moment, he was holding Bedwyr upright, long legs planted wide, one hand gentling his ribs. Bedwyr hummed at the touch. As good as this was, here and upright, how would that same touch feel in the comfort of their bed? Callused fingertips roving lightly on his bare skin…

"I want you," he said on a rush.

Arthur growled into his mouth.

A third person cleared their throat.

He jerked away from Arthur, and they turned toward the path. Gwen stood there, arms crossed, head tipped to one side.

Bedwyr swiped at his mouth, and his sister smirked.

"Training, eh?" Her eyes flicked from him to Arthur and back. "No wonder you two are so hungry."

She strode past them into the hut. Bedwyr shrugged off his shield and followed her. Arthur's tall presence darkened the doorway behind him, pressing him toward Gwen, who was taking things from her basket. Cheese, bread, apples, walnuts. She set them one by one on the small table. Between her silence and Arthur's, he could scarcely breathe. Then she held up a wrapped parcel.

"Brought you a sweet cake, but it seems you've discovered something sweeter." She gave them that scrutinizing look again.

They shuffled like two errant apprentices, and she set it on the table with the rest.

"So?" she said.

Bedwyr watched her calm movements, envying them. "So, what?"

She turned and leaned against the table. "Truly? I come upon you kissing and it's *so, what?*"

"It was just a kiss," he said.

She stared at him with their father's eyes. "Forgive me, big brother, I've not known you to dole them out."

"It was me," Arthur cut in. "I started it. Bed was pushing me off."

Gwen studied him and then cocked an eyebrow at Bedwyr. "Is that true?"

Arthur was giving him an out. Would Gwen believe it? The hut felt overly warm.

"I won't tell anyone," Gwen said softly.

He looked away, ashamed at having waited for her reassurance. "It's not true. I wasn't pushing him away."

"Good." When he looked back, surprised, she was smiling. "It's about time you went along willingly." She giggled. "Wouldn't Eira be livid."

"Gwen—"

"I *won't*." She sighed and turned to the table again. "She's just so full of herself."

He looked at Arthur, who shrugged. "She is full of herself. What's she do besides fuck a warlord?"

"And brag about it," Gwen muttered.

He couldn't care less. "Heard you broke Cai's finger."

"He was acting the arse," she said, stirring the little pot of goat's cheese. "As usual."

"He came here."

She turned to him, expression now wary.

"He didn't see anything."

Her shoulders seemed to relax. "I'm sorry, Bedwyr. I shouldn't have told him. I only wanted to make him stop."

"Next time," Arthur said, "knee him in the stones."

She gave him a worried smile. "Doesn't that hurt?"

"You broke his finger."

She shrugged. "Hurt more, I mean?"

"It's different," Arthur said. "He'll think twice about bothering you."

Bothering her. Bedwyr's teeth ground the thought to grit. If he'd been around, Cai never would have tried it. "Tell Ta," he said.

"He told me to knee Cai in the stones." She grinned, then looked back and forth between them. "So…when did it start?"

"When did what start?" Bedwyr asked, uneasy.

She pursed her lips and made kissing noises at him.

"Right." Arthur stepped around him and opened the door. "Thanks for dropping in, Gwen."

"Oh, come," she said, "I brought you sweet cake. Please?" She gave Bedwyr an imploring look. "One little detail?"

"His armpits are ticklish," Arthur said and gestured her out.

"Pfff. Even I know that." She gathered her basket and made to leave. Just past the posts, she turned and fluttered her eyelashes at Arthur. "Still, can't help but notice none of *your* fingers are broken."

Arthur shoved the door into place and leaned back against it.

They listened as Gwen's low chuckling receded, and then Arthur gave him a weary smile.

"At least I won the sweet cake wager."

CHAPTER 15

It was dark when Bedwyr arrived at the smithy.

After Gwen's interrogation, he and Arthur had been more cautious. They'd continued sparring, eaten some bread, napped apart, then practiced again. When the sun had begun to set, Arthur left to enlist his mother's help, and Bedwyr had grown increasingly restless. Gwen wouldn't tell anyone about the kiss, least of all their father. But the prospect of going back into the village made him feel even more exposed now that someone else knew.

With nothing to do in the empty smithy but wait, he leaned against the workbench. In his day, Arthur's grandfather Wolf had run this workshop. He'd been a bear of a man, taller than anyone in the village and broader even than Uthyr. Like Master Matthias, his son, Master Wolf had had hair the color of winter grass, though his beard was already gray when Bedwyr met him. If it was daylight, Master Wolf had worn his leather apron, his great hammer swinging from a loop on his belt. He'd been a calm, good-natured presence, and Bedwyr had wished often that Cai were closer to the smith. If he had been, Bedwyr could have spent more time in his company. The dagger he wore at his belt was one Master Wolf had made. When Bedwyr and Cai had returned from their first patrol and had their inking ceremony, Arthur had presented them with twin daggers. Master Wolf claimed Arthur had designed them, but he knew the old smith had forged them himself.

In light of what Arthur had said about his grandfather's acceptance of him, he was glad Arthur had had the man to confide in. It made sense that Master Wolf had assumed Bedwyr would be uninterested. Who would think the blood son of Uthyr would desire other men? Or even admit it if he did? He'd been only four when Arthur's family had arrived with Masters Tiro and Philip, but he remembered the consternation over the marriage-like bond between Marcus and Wolf, and the less formal but equally tenacious partnership shared by Tiro and Master Philip. Each man had proven his worth to the community, but murmurings about their private lives lingered. For Bedwyr to admit to wanting such a bond would have risked his inheritance of his father's seat of power.

To his father, such a succession was no longer possible. Was he a fool to have any hope of changing Uthyr's mind?

A scuff outside and low voices brought him back to the present. Two dark shapes stepped into the workshop.

"Bed?"

"Yeah."

Mistress Britte lit a twig from the banked coals of the fire pan and held it to the wick of a lantern until it caught. Setting the lantern on the workbench, she turned to him and nodded.

"Bedwyr."

"Mistress."

"How are you?"

It took him a moment to make sense of the words. He couldn't remember her asking him that before. "I'm well. Thank you."

One corner of her mouth pinched. "Glad to hear it. Let's have the shield."

He set it on the workbench, and she began to untack some of the straps.

Nearly as tall as Arthur's father, but stouter, the blacksmith was a formidable woman. His own father, who treated most women as lower creatures, made by the gods to do his household work and sexual bidding, treated Mistress Britte with a respect that was almost cautious. Word was that she had known Master Wolf since she was a small girl and had apprenticed to him before marrying his son. He had given over the running of the smithy to her some years before, and she had run it since.

Bedwyr didn't remember who had smithed before Arthur's family had arrived, but visitors to the village often commented on the work that came out of this shop. The sword that Master Marcus had carried had been extraordinary. He had let Bedwyr hold it once, and once only. It had felt substantial yet light, a trick of its balance. Its dark gray blade had held ripples in it, as if Master Wolf had trapped a river in the steel during its forging.

Cai had wanted the sword, badly—his first tattoo had been a rendering of the blade. But when Master Marcus died, confusion arose over who had been promised the weapon, with Cai and Arthur each making a loud claim. In the end, Mistress Britte had declared it would be entombed with Marcus Roman, to lie between the man who had created it and the one who had carried it.

No one, not even Uthyr, had dared suggest otherwise.

"Hold up your arm."

When Mistress Britte said a thing, the thing happened. He held up his arm.

"Arthur, take the weight."

Arthur stepped forward and, gripping the shield's rim, held it in front of Bedwyr. It put them face to face, scarcely two feet apart, and the cub took full advantage. As his mother refitted the harness, her full attention on the arrangement of the leather strapping, Arthur kept Bedwyr trained on him. On his plump bottom lip. On the slow swipe of his tongue over it, leaving it glistening in the lamplight like a piece of summer fruit. On his throat when he tipped his head to one side to crack his neck. When Bedwyr tried to look away, Arthur's fingers tapped the edge of the shield, calling him back like a wayward puppy.

Stop, Bedwyr mouthed.

Arthur's lips quirked. *Make me.*

I'll do it.

Oooo, how?

"That's as much as I can do without trapping you—" Mistress Britte broke off and looked closely at Bedwyr. "Are you all right?"

He cleared his throat. "I'm fine."

"You're flushed."

Behind her, Arthur was smirking. He wiped it away just as she turned to him, giving her an innocent look.

"Humph." She gave one final squint before rounding on Bedwyr. "You still need to be able to shed it quickly, yes?"

"Yes, Mistress."

Arthur winked at him.

He glared back.

"Step onto the path outside to see how it handles. Here." She handed him a short sword from a pile of weapons to be repaired. "Arthur, take a blade and face him."

"Yes, Commander."

"Don't be sly," she said softly.

"Don't be shy, either."

They all turned at the grate of Uthyr's voice.

He stepped into the workshop, thumbs tucked into his belt. "I saw a light from the meeting hall and wondered what could be keeping our good smith away from the story fire and Tiro's latest tale."

Mistress Britte said nothing.

Uthyr looked at Bedwyr and the shield he wore. "You've been training?"

He straightened his shoulders. "Yes."

"Well." Uthyr waved toward the walkway outside. "Show me."

Here it was: his opportunity. He walked onto the dim path in front of the workshop. The sword felt unfamiliar in his grasp, and he wished he'd thought to bring his own. The new straps of the shield were tight around the pulse in his short arm. His mind raced as he took up a neutral stance on the dark path outside, over-aware of his father's assessing gaze on him. What did he see?

Arthur cleared his throat. Bedwyr looked at him just as he planted his feet opposite. The slant of light from the smithy just allowed him to see Arthur's face. Holding Bedwyr's eye, he slowly rolled his shoulders. When Bedwyr followed suit, Arthur gave him a small nod.

Bedwyr charged.

He tried to forget his father was watching, that the sword wasn't his, that the shield harness was untested. He struck, and Arthur blocked. Arthur swung, and he fended off the blow. It was only the two of them, he told himself. Only the two of them, and they were outside the shepherd's hut, circling each other on the bit of muddy ground whose snow and grass they'd trampled over the past several weeks. No one was watching him but Arthur. Nothing mattered but the angle of Arthur's next strike and the opportunity it would open up to him.

He took them all, those moments when Arthur reached too far or exposed a leg, a rib, his neck, leaving them vulnerable to Bedwyr's approach. And because he faced Arthur, Bedwyr gave up opportunities, too. His partner was long but fast, and thoroughly tested his ability to defend himself from crown to heel. Once, Arthur followed a low swipe with a high downswing so quickly Bedwyr nearly didn't lift his shield in time to deflect the blow. But he did—just—and fed his cub some immediate retribution. Arthur's teeth flashed at him, glinting with pride, and he was invincible.

Their clashing armor rang in the cool air. They should spar at night more often—set up a couple of lanterns and have at. Let the shadows show them something new, let the gods hear the songs of their blades. He grinned at the thought and threw his shield forward, driving Arthur's sword sideways and Arthur himself backward. The younger man tripped on his own feet and went down.

Bedwyr stood over him for a moment, panting, his breath forming a cloud between them. Arthur grinned up at him, a smile too bright to be dimmed by anything so insubstantial as steam. Bedwyr held out his hand, and Arthur pulled himself up with a groan.

"Impressive."

In one word his father's voice broke the illusion of a solitary match.

"You left little more than a month ago," Uthyr said to him.

Was sent away was closer to the truth, but he nodded.

Uthyr turned to Arthur. "Good work, young man. And you were fighting left-handed."

Arthur looked at Bedwyr. "We decided to level the yard, so to speak."

"We...or you?"

Arthur frowned, then said, "We."

"Hmm." Uthyr didn't sound convinced. "You should take the credit you've earned. I set you an impossible task."

Bedwyr felt himself rock on his feet. *Impossible task.*

"When I sent you after him, I wasn't sure what would come of it. I half expected to have to come do the job myself."

Arthur's eyes were wide in the dark, flashing toward Bedwyr. "H-he took to it right away. He's your son, my lord. It's in his blood. He nearly always bested me, just like before."

Bedwyr stared at him. He'd forgotten how to breathe, and his lungs had begun to ache with it.

Uthyr turned to him. "I also told him not to tell you I sent him."

One black eyebrow rose. "Did he?"

Arthur's throat contracted on a hard swallow.

Something curdled in Bedwyr's gut. Arthur had spent the past weeks at the tiny hut on Uthyr's order. He hadn't come out of guilt, or any sense of responsibility. He hadn't come out of friendship or been compelled by the bond of brotherhood among fighting men. He certainly hadn't come out of a desire to spend time with him. To share his bed.

Gods, it had all been some tale Arthur had fed him—what lad began to want another at ten years of age? How would someone as mouthy as Arthur keep such a secret for the eight years since? He couldn't have done so. He hadn't had to do so, because there'd been no secret. No wanting, no hiding. No perceptive, supportive grandfather. No such desire at all. It would have been laughable if it hadn't been so fucking mortifying. Had he cringed at the sensation of Bedwyr's stump under his head? Felt trapped by him on the coldest nights? Shuddered with disgust at his hand—his mouth, his seed—on his body?

Bedwyr stepped backward.

Uthyr turned back to Arthur. "I'll take that as confirmation."

Arthur's gaze seemed to swim with guilt, though Bedwyr didn't now trust himself to judge these things. He tugged the shield off his shoulder and turned to Mistress Britte. She was glaring at Uthyr. *Don't waste your effort,* he wanted to tell her. "Thank you for your help, Mistress."

She turned to him, frowning. "Of course."

Numbly, he set the sword on the workbench. The lamps threw the jittering shadow of the hilt against the scarred wooden surface.

"Bedwyr."

His right shoulder jerked reflexively against his father's voice, causing the loosened shield to knock his thigh. He hitched it up on his arm. He didn't want to face him, but ignoring that voice was an impossibility, trained out of him by the time he'd learned to walk.

The man's eyes looked like bottomless black pools. "I sent you away to spare you humiliation."

"To spare me, or you?" he said without thinking.

Uthyr's eyes narrowed, and Bedwyr's breath snagged in his throat. He'd never contradicted his father, and now he'd done so in front of others. In front of Mistress Britte.

That must have stung.

Uthyr crossed the smithy silently. When he stood before him, close and seething, Bedwyr had to fight the urge to take a step backward. "I've held this region for a long time," Uthyr said in a low, controlled voice that belied his anger. "But don't imagine there aren't five different gambits for power being discussed at this moment, behind my back. Any show of weakness, including you having to relearn sword craft, would only fuel their fires."

Bedwyr wanted to believe him. Men were bound to talk, especially during the long, idle months of winter. Maybe his father truly had been protecting their house, Bedwyr's own birthright. Despite his many flaws, his father had been the most solid presence in his life, always near, always leading the way, always training him. He had, for better or worse, equipped Bedwyr to survive, and to survive him.

Still, one thing niggled at him. "Why was Arthur not to tell me you sent him?"

Uthyr's nostrils flared. After a long moment, he said, "That was part of his punishment."

All the air left Bedwyr's lungs. There it was. It hadn't been about rehabilitating him, or restoring him in any way, with witnesses or without. He'd only been an instrument in some scheme of justice. A means to ensure that one bright but reckless young warrior didn't make the same mistake twice.

Mistress Britte stepped toward him. "Bedwyr—"

He shook his head, unable to speak. Ducking away, he strode quickly from the workshop.

"Bed," Arthur called, "*wait*."

Ignoring that voice was imperative.

With his own name ringing in his ears, he fled back up the dark path.

~

He was pacing behind the hut when Arthur showed up.

Stilling his footsteps, he listened as the cub entered the hut. His voice carried in the chill air—agitated, pitched higher than usual. When it was no longer muffled by the hut, Bedwyr edged close to the rear wall and pressed his back to the building.

As he'd expected, Arthur rounded the small structure, the crunch of his boots in the snow preceding his tall form, but not by much. He strode quickly toward the stream and called out.

"Bed!"

The sound of it jabbed at his ribs. He waited under the eave, scarcely breathing.

"Bed, please. Let me explain!"

Explain what? That everything had been a lie. That was too clear now—no explanation needed.

Arthur waited longer for a response, but as time passed and none came, his hands curled into fists. "It wasn't a trick, I swear it!"

The cold, hard wall of the hut chilled Bedwyr's back. He imagined it freezing his body—spine, then limbs, then his jaw—so that he stayed rooted to his hiding place, unable to move or speak. The cold was having trouble reaching the center of his chest, though; it burned as though a small, live coal rested there, glowing sullenly.

Arthur turned and walked to the fire pit. With a growl that sounded frustrated, he kicked at the ashes. He stared at the dark smudge they left on the surrounding snow.

"It wasn't a trick," he said, more subdued. Then he turned and rounded the hut once more.

Bedwyr waited, listening. Arthur entered the hut again, and Bedwyr cursed. The cub was going to wait him out again, just as he'd done when he'd shown himself weeks ago. He knew the cold would drive Bedwyr inside eventually. For an upstart, he had an unfortunate patient streak.

But then another sound drifted around to him, one he'd grown so accustomed to he could have plucked it from a crowd of noises: the knocking of Arthur's scabbard on his shield. Then more now-familiar sounds: the door being shoved back into place, a quiet "Fuck," and Arthur's footfalls—he knew them so well they seemed to live under his skin. Except that now Arthur wasn't waiting for Bedwyr, as he'd done before. He was leaving.

Bedwyr stared at the marred fire pit far longer than it would take the man to walk away from the hut, down the path, and back to the warm hearth of his parents' house. Back to his people and his life. Back to Uthyr and his plans.

He waited, watching the moon track a cold path over the snow.

When the coal in the center of his chest gave up the last of its light, he left his place under the eave and went inside.

CHAPTER 16

The next day was long without training.

Bedwyr hadn't realized how many hours they'd passed circling each other outside. Enough that little snow remained on that trampled grass.

Arthur's boot prints were everywhere else, though. Near the fire pit, along the stream bank to his fish traps, in a jumble at the woodpile. Bedwyr scuffed them all, wanted to erase any record of the cub's presence. As many as he swiped with his own boot, more seemed to appear, until he gave up and trudged back inside.

The hut was dark and too quiet. No, strike that—it was exactly as dark and quiet as he wanted it to be. Finally, he'd have the peace he'd wanted weeks ago. No early morning chatter, no blinding glare of firelight on naked skin. He'd have the food to himself. The bed to himself. The entire ramshackle place to himself, damn the thing. With a triumphant grunt, he grabbed a hunk of bread from the table and tore into it.

After gnashing his teeth for several seconds, he stepped outside to spit it out. When had Gwen started baking sawdust into it?

Disgruntled, he sat down on one of the stumps and stared at the hearth. It lay empty but for ash. A draft down the short chimney stirred the pale stuff into a wisp that rose briefly, twisting into something like a lock of hair before settling again. A faint whistle sounded around the door as a northerly wind swept around the hut. The log under him creaked, then fell silent.

If it was going to be so quiet maybe he would take advantage.

He'd had precious few naps over the past month and more. No time for naps when there was sparring to do or fresh-caught fish to eat or groping hands to capture. Crossing to the bunk, he lay down. The blankets wrestled with his boots until he kicked the woolen fabric more or less into submission. He closed his eyes.

copper-fire hair

His eyes snapped open. The low rafters hung sullenly above him, devoid of color. He tried again. Tugging one willing blanket to his chest, he let his eyes fall shut.

And...peace. Nothing but the blessed hush of a shepherd's hut in winter.

Gripping the blanket, he tried to settle in, only now the mattress felt strange, poking his back and legs in every annoying way it could muster, as if he hadn't been sleeping on it since midwinter. Frustrated, he rolled onto his side.

The ticking bent under him exactly as it should, as it had for weeks. There was the table, there the hearth. But then things began to feel lacking. His short arm, crooked in front of him, supporting nothing. His other arm, accustomed to resting on a warm body, lay limp at his belt.

He closed his eyes again, and this time he let the impressions come. The rise and fall of Arthur's ribs against his fingers. The weight of his head on his biceps. The brush of his hair across Bedwyr's nose and the sharp smoky scent of the strands.

With dread in his belly but unable to stop himself, he drew a long, seeking breath...and smelled nothing.

The emptiness he'd been trying to ignore wasn't at the fire pit or in the dim hut, or even in the bunk. It lay in his middle, like a great hole that sucked all sensation into its maw—the sounds, the scents, the warmth.

It had been phantom, all of it, conjured solely to fulfill a warlord's scheme. Bedwyr had only been unlucky enough to experience the spell.

Swallowing his disappointment, he rolled over and stared at the wall.

~

The sun rose and fell, but Bedwyr didn't care. He no longer

needed it.

No need for light when all a fool did was lie on his side, facing the cracked daub of a wall and thinking of nothing.

Nothing tasted right. Nothing sounded right. Nothing smelled right.

His world was nothing, and none of it was right. Yet the sun kept on making its shallow, cloud-muted arc.

Stubborn.

Gwen said as much when she appeared during one interminable gray day, though she might not have been talking about the sun.

She made it very difficult to do the important work of thinking of nothing, as she clucked about food and blankets, and scuffled around the hearth to build a fire. Did nobody understand? He didn't need fire. Once, he had been fire. Now he wasn't. His body had let it go out.

"You're freezing."

He wasn't, but Gwen wouldn't listen and lay down behind him anyway. And so he had to endure being wrapped up in warmth from a body too short, too soft, and being scolded by a voice too much not the one he was trying not to think about.

Eventually, Gwen slipped away, and so did the sun.

~

Bedwyr lay in the dark when a knock sounded on the door.
Gods' blood.
"Piss off," he moaned.

The door shifted. Lantern light shone around its edges, and Bedwyr growled at the thought of being forced into sight. He rose and stalked toward the door, ready to turn his sister around and send her right back to their father—at least Uthyr still claimed her as his own—but he stopped short as his visitor ducked through.

Master Matthias smiled at him. "Always with the warm welcome."

Bedwyr took an unsteady step backward.

The healer set his case on the table, his smile turning downward then as he looked at the hearth. "You've no fire."

"Don't need one."

Matthias took hold of his arms, his large hands chafing Bedwyr's sleeves. "You'll freeze."

"I won't."

The healer shook his head and stepped away. Now Bedwyr's arms *were* cold.

He watched the man kneel before the hearth but didn't have the energy to stop his industry. Before long, a small fire crackled there, warming his right side.

Matthias rose, ducking to avoid the beams, and stepped back toward him. "I came to check your arm."

"It's fine."

Matthias shrugged. "I'm a bit chilled from the walk, and the fire feels good. Humor me?"

Without waiting for Bedwyr's response, which seemed lodged in his throat anyway, Matthias arranged the two log stumps that served as seats and gestured him to take one. Unable to say why he did so—why he didn't just leave the hut and start walking across the snowy hills—Bedwyr sat.

Matthias lowered himself onto the other stump with a sigh and flicked his fingers. "Let's see that arm."

"It's healed."

"With all due respect to your expertise, I'll make my own judgment."

It was as close to a rebuke as Master Matthias had ever given him, even when he and Cai had wreaked mischief as boys. Bedwyr held out his right arm.

Nimbly, Matthias pulled the pin that gathered the extra sleeve and slipped it through his own. Then he rolled up Bedwyr's to expose his arm and began to examine him. Despite his claim of being chilled from the walk, his hands were warm. Bedwyr watched the man's fingers press and prod his skin. They were long and blunt-nailed, extending from broad palms and strong wrists. Yet their touch was gentle, and not in a hesitant way that might frustrate.

There was a confidence in Matthias's touch, a sureness that spoke of experience and of knowledge earned. Matthias's hands roved up and down his arm, his thumbs smoothing the width of Bedwyr's scar. Then he stopped, simply cradling his forearm. Bedwyr looked up to find the man watching him.

"How are you, Bedwyr?"

In the receding chill of the air, Matthias's soft voice wrapped Bedwyr's shoulders like a blanket. His voice was pitched low, as if he knew that, in this small space, he needn't speak any louder for Bedwyr to hear him. To understand him. He looked at Matthias more closely. The man's brown eyes held his own intently. The fire made the hair at his temples look especially fine and picked out the silver in his short beard. His lips rested calmly, patiently.

Bedwyr leaned forward and kissed him.

At first, he noticed only that Matthias's lips were soft, the queue of his hair smooth where Bedwyr held his neck.

But then it crept in, what was missing. The press of nose and teeth. An eagerly responsive tongue. A certain apple-like flavor. The healer wasn't moving, wasn't making a sound.

And he wasn't the person Bedwyr wanted to be kissing. He froze, mortified into immobility.

Those warm hands came to rest on his face and drew him away gently.

Bedwyr closed his eyes. "I'm sorry." What had he done to find himself in such tight quarters with a man for whom he'd carried a ridiculous soft spot since boyhood? If he wished hard enough, would he go away?

"Bedwyr."

"Please don't tell anyone."

"Look at me."

Reluctantly he did.

Matthias's eyes shone back at him. "There's no shame in it."

He wanted to shrivel up with shame nonetheless.

"Have you forgotten who my fathers were?"

"I shouldn't have done it. I'm sorry."

"Lad." Matthias smiled. "Things get tangled sometimes. And other times..." He studied Bedwyr's face. "Other times they unspool unexpectedly. That was a long time coming, was it not?"

His instinct to shrink came back. "You knew?"

"I suspected," Matthias said softly. "I've known you for a long time."

As a boy. As a stupid pup. Bedwyr pulled away.

Matthias laid a hand on his. "I would say I'm grateful you tried on me; most other men here would have balked. Harmed you, possibly. But I wasn't the first, was I?"

Steeling himself, Bedwyr said, "No. Not the first."

"Not even the first of my house," Matthias said quietly. "Quite the tangle."

Bedwyr looked up to find a strange quirk about the healer's mouth.

He knew about Arthur. How much did he know? Had Arthur told him? And this hut, this cramped, humid space. Could Matthias tell that Bedwyr had coaxed the man's son into his bed with selfish motives and then stroked and sucked until he shouted? The blankets were stained with their seed. Could Master Matthias smell it? Healers supposedly had keen senses of smell. Their vocation demanded it—

Matthias squeezed his hand, then sat back. "The arm seems to be coming along. It's good that you've had so much exercise."

Was that all he was going to say?

"But there are other considerations."

That quirk of the mouth again. "Considerations?"

"For a start, your plans for continued training."

"Training's over."

"Oh? My father gave me the impression it was a lifetime's work."

It was, for most. "Not for me."

Master Matthias scanned the hut. "There's also the matter of how you'll be feeding yourself. Nourishment is important to healing."

"Gwen brings meals."

"Does she?" Matthias considered that. "How long do you suppose she'll be able to do that? Surely she'll marry someday soon."

"I'll feed myself."

"How?"

"I'll fish."

"Do you plan to tend the sheep too, because if not, I predict the shepherd boys will need their hut back come spring."

Would no one leave him to his misery? "Are we finished?"

Master Matthias pulled himself back. He gave a thoughtful nod. "I have only one more question for you. I promise it's relevant."

"And that is?"

Matthias looked at him closely. "Can you forgive my son?"

The question landed like a blow under the ribs.

"Let me be more specific, because Arthur has, perhaps, done more than one thing requiring forgiveness—"

"It wasn't his fault," he blurted. "My hand, I mean."

The master's smile was gentle. "Ah, Bedwyr, even I know Arthur was at fault. Not only did he ignore his training, he did so within view of you."

"What does that mean?"

"You're rather protective of him. You've been that way since he was very young. If not for you, Cai might have strangled Arthur before his balls dropped."

Bedwyr snorted, surprised to hear such common words from the healer.

"I know my sons," Matthias said. "And I know your contribution toward the men they've become. Right down to the ink on their arms."

"Arthur doesn't have ink."

Master Matthias gave him a curious look.

"And he lied." He didn't like saying so to the man, but it sat in the room with them, the truth of the lie.

"I know." Matthias frowned at the lantern. "Did he tell you Lord Uthyr threatened him with banishment if he didn't succeed in restoring you?"

Gods. "No."

"He only just told his mother and me." He looked back to Bedwyr. "It's a strange thing to come so close to losing a child and not fully understand until after the danger's passed."

"I'm sorry."

"No, I'm sorry. That's not your burden to carry. I'm sure Uthyr had his reasons, and I can't argue with the effectiveness of his methods. Britte says you're a force to reckon with again."

"If Mistress Britte says so."

"Indeed."

He hadn't been alone in front of the smithy, though. Would he have done as well had his father sent Huw to the shepherd's hut, or Tiro, or even Cai? He might have tried just to please the older men. And while Cai was a friend, he wasn't sure he could have overcome the doubt in Cai's eyes. But Arthur had made him want to try, and for himself.

Had that been only a tactic to meet Uthyr's demands, or had there been more to it in Arthur's mind?

"That was Arthur's doing too," he said, "what my father saw. What Mistress Britte saw."

"It takes two men to spar, and don't bother arguing that. My father tried to train me to arms, but I didn't want it. What Britte saw the other night was a young man who does want it. Was she mistaken?"

"No."

Matthias nodded. "Only Arthur can answer for his actions, and only to you. But I believe he would have come to you whether Uthyr had ordered him to or not. Arthur…admires you, very much. I don't expect you to hold him at the same level of regard. Frankly, I'm not sure that's possible."

It was possible. The coal in Bedwyr's chest began to flicker.

"I hope you can let him try to be a friend." Matthias sighed. "It's the least he can do to repay the years of kindness you've shown him."

Kindness. Was that what he'd dealt Arthur?

Matthias stood and collected his case and lantern. Bedwyr followed him to the door, where Matthias turned to him.

"Promise me one thing, Bedwyr."

"What?"

"Keep the fire burning."

Bedwyr watched him make his way toward the village in his small ring of light. When he disappeared around the shoulder of the hillside, Bedwyr shifted the door back into place. Then he lay down facing the hearth and pulled the blankets up to his nose, daring Arthur's scent to find him.

CHAPTER 17

Arthur sat hunched in the meeting hall as everyone else listened to Tiro's tale for the evening.

His neighbors had been curious when he'd reappeared in the village three days before. Word had gotten 'round in his absence—thanks to Cai, most likely—that he'd been training with Bedwyr. Several people stopped him at his chores to ask how Bedwyr fared. The warriors among them wanted to know if Bed had been able to handle a sword left-handed. A few thanked Arthur for what they'd mistaken as his own initiative to redress the grief he'd wrought on Bedwyr's life.

When he told them it'd been Lord Uthyr's idea, they had nodded their heads at the justice in the warlord's decision, so Master Philip had been right about that. Arthur didn't tell them Bedwyr had been unaware of the scheme. And he would never let on to what they'd discovered about each other.

It didn't matter now anyway. He'd failed. Not Lord Uthyr—no, he had come through on that. Bedwyr could fight again. He needed more practice, and he might never be as adept with his left hand as his right, but he could handle a sword. With more work, he would get the hang of the shield harness too.

Arthur had failed Bedwyr. He'd gotten into the hut through pity, bullied the man into training, even lit a fuse he hadn't known Bedwyr possessed. He'd worked his way into Bedwyr's confidence and then failed to confide in him. Sure, he'd shared some things about himself, about his grandfathers…but he hadn't shared the most important thing: that he had wanted to be there and not because he'd been ordered to do so.

He hadn't seen Bedwyr in three days, hadn't felt him for three nights. He wasn't sure which he missed more.

"You look miserable."

Gwen stood over him. He shrugged.

She made a sound of disgust and sat down beside him. "Men."

Oh, here they went.

"You're such moaners," she said, even though he hadn't asked.

"Moaners?"

"Yes, moaners." She pulled a grumpy face. "'I'm not hungry. I'm not lonely. My arm does *not* hurt.'"

His arm— Arthur straightened. "Is he in pain?"

"Of course he's in pain, Arthur." She looked at him closely. "But it isn't his arm that's hurting him."

He looked away. "What else would it be?"

"What else? Let's see…" She began to tick off possibilities with her fingertips. "His feet? No, those are as big and galumphing as ever."

Bed needed big feet. He was a large fellow.

"His gut? No, can't be, unless it's hunger pangs from not eating."

"He's not eating?"

She narrowed her eyes at him. "Is it his head? Hmm, could be. He's grumbling enough to give any fool a headache."

"Grumbling about what?"

"What isn't he grumbling about? The fire's too cold. The wind keeps him awake. The thatch smells rank."

He tried to imagine stoic Bedwyr complaining about all those things and couldn't help but smile.

Gwen poked him in the shoulder. "It's not kind to enjoy other people's pain."

"Where's he hurting, Gwen?"

"Where do you suppose, Arthur?" When he didn't answer, she jabbed at his breastbone. "Same place you're hurting, you lump."

"He's got a cough?"

She made a loud sound of frustration, loud enough to draw a few inquiring glances. They turned into indulgent smiles. To the room, they probably looked like young lovers.

Little did his neighbors know.

"Fine," he said. "You're right."

Gwen crowed, drawing more interested glances.

"So what do I do about it?" Arthur said. "He thinks I lied to him."

"You did."

"Nothing I said was a lie."

"No, only everything you didn't say." She looked at him closely. "Right?"

It had always been this way, as if she could read his mind as easily as one of Master Philip's scrolls. Why didn't the ability go both ways?

But he couldn't deny that Gwen had the right of it. He needed to go to Bedwyr and tell him everything. "Do you think he'll listen to me?"

"You made yourself a nuisance once before, and he let you in."

"Eventually."

"Isn't it worth it?"

It was. He would camp outside the hut as long as it took.

Arthur stood and had taken two steps toward the entrance of the hall when a cry arose.

"Lord Uthyr!"

The hall fell quiet at the call from the doorway. The scout Gwilym stood there, breathing hard. Uthyr rose from his chair.

"What is it?"

"Saxons," Gwilym said. "Five miles distant."

The hall erupted.

Gwen grabbed his arm. "You know what to do now, right?"

He did.

By the time he reached the shepherd's hut, his side was stitched as tightly as if his father had sewn him up. He shouldered the door open with a hard shove.

Bedwyr sprang up from one of the log stumps, dagger drawn.

"Saxon raiders, five miles."

Bedwyr stared at him, wide-eyed. "I…"

"You need to fight."

"I can't."

He crossed the hut and grabbed the man's shoulders. "You can."

"Uthyr doesn't want me."

"He sent me."

"Are you lying?"

"Yes."

Bedwyr frowned. "What?"

Arthur gripped him. "I'm sorry. For not telling you your father sent me before. I should have told you. I owed you that much."

Bedwyr shook his head. "I've barely used the shield," he said, as if Arthur had said nothing. "For all I know it'll fall off. I'd be going into a fight with a few weeks training."

He wasn't going to hear Arthur's apology. Fine. That was his right. But he was wrong about the rest of it. "You've trained your whole life, Bed. It's in you. Here"—he punched the man's shoulder—"and here"—he kicked his boot—"and here"—he smacked his head.

Bedwyr raised a hand to his head and rubbed. "Ow."

Arthur poked him in the chest. "And it's in here."

Bedwyr smacked his hand away. "Save your flowering verse, poet."

"You need to do this."

"I'm a liability."

"You're not—"

"Leave me be—"

"*I* need you to do this," Arthur blurted, desperation clawing at his back.

"Why?" Bedwyr scowled. "So you can get your ink?"

"No, you arsehole! Because I've been training with my left fucking hand for a month and now you're the only shieldmate I know how to fight with!"

It wasn't true and Bedwyr knew it, was glaring at him. "Just switch hands," he said. "It'll come back."

"Same to you."

The man's jaw worked, his expression wavering between retort and something Arthur couldn't suss. That he was about to get hit was a likely possibility.

But Bedwyr didn't strike him. "Sparring with each other and fighting side by side are two different things."

He couldn't fail Bed again—there was too much at stake. "I'll do whatever you tell me to do."

A harsh laugh grated from Bedwyr's throat.

"I will."

Dark eyes drilled into him for long seconds. "Swear it."

"You have my word."

A tilt of Bedwyr's head said Arthur's word rested on swampy

ground.

"I swear it, Bed."

Bedwyr looked at him, his gaze searching Arthur's face. He didn't seem convinced, and Arthur couldn't blame him. But after a few seconds, he bent to where his sword and shield rested against the wall of the hut and hefted them. "Let's go."

~

The crowd at the armory quieted as they walked toward Lord Uthyr. Arthur led the way, trying to keep his shoulders square and confident. Moments like this one made him glad for his height; it carried with it an authority he didn't fully understand yet but had often seen reflected on the faces of people who spoke to his father, or to his grandfathers in their day.

It also allowed him to see everyone's faces, and just now they all were staring at Bedwyr, their eyes flicking between his face and someplace lower—his stump, most likely. Their uncertainty was something Arthur could almost smell, and it made him want to use his body to shield Bedwyr.

But Bedwyr wouldn't welcome that, not here.

Lord Uthyr watched them approach. When they neared the workbench where he stood, Bedwyr stepped up beside Arthur.

The warlord leveled a hard look at his son. "You want to fight?"

"Yes."

Uthyr examined him in a brow-to-boot sweep that would have made Arthur want to jump out of his skin. Bedwyr bore the scrutiny, a slight tightness around his eyes the only sign that it affected him. At length, Lord Uthyr nodded curtly. "Cai!"

"My lord?"

"Your shieldmate has returned."

Arthur flinched at Uthyr's words. But worse was the obvious doubt in Cai's eyes when he looked at Bed.

"I fight with Arthur," Bedwyr said.

Cai's eyes snapped to meet Arthur's, and he couldn't help lifting his chin, just a bit, in satisfaction.

After a moment, Lord Uthyr said, "Very well," and the men went back to readying their gear.

When they left the armory, Arthur fell in behind Bedwyr. From his position, he could see little sign of Bed's injury. Between the shield on his back, his winter cloak, and the night's darkness, a fellow might miss it. Training had kept Bedwyr's shoulders broad and powerful. He walked with his spine straight and head up, and Arthur hoped the training had done that too. The only thing that gave away the change in the man's condition was the cant of his scabbard, positioned now to draw using his left hand.

The Saxons' location was a few hours' hike through snow, but the Cymry made the walk in silence. It seemed to suit Bed, but Arthur wished someone would say something. Anything would have sufficed, even just a low song to help pass the miles.

If he were honest with himself, he didn't care what the other men said or didn't—he wanted Bedwyr to speak. They walked in the middle of the queue of men, and Arthur regretted not contriving some reason for them to bring up the rear. Maybe then he might have gotten a bit of conversation out of Bed. Idle chatter, a joke, anything.

Well, not just anything. He was bound for battle and could have used some advice. Bed shouldn't have to advise him—not when Arthur had caused his injury in the first place—but seeking out Tiro for encouraging words would undermine what he'd worked to give Bedwyr. He wanted the men to have the same confidence in Bedwyr that Arthur had. According to Gwen, no one had been all that surprised when Lord Uthyr had sent him to train with Bedwyr. They *had* been taken aback when Bed announced he would fight alongside Arthur tonight. But Bedwyr's stalwart determination had convinced them. Now Arthur had to walk behind him, questions unanswered, lest anyone sense the gaping chasm between them. He hoped they could bridge it long enough to survive a skirmish.

What he really wanted to do was steer Bed into the trees and have everything out skin to skin, cold or no, but some things couldn't be had just for the wishing of them.

As he crunched through the trampled snow, he tried his grandfather's trick and mentally upended all his competing thoughts onto the moonlit ground. Then, one by one, he sorted them back into two jars: useful and not.

~

The Saxons had camped under the cover of forest. Lord Uthyr signaled a halt half a mile short of their quarry. The scouts moved ahead to intercept the invaders' sentries.

Arthur helped Bedwyr don the shield harness and tighten the straps. When Bedwyr sat on a log to wait, Arthur looked around at the other warriors. To a man, they were settling in for naps. He rolled his shoulders, restless. "How can you sit?"

"Simple. On my arse."

"Funny."

Bedwyr's expression showed no humor. "About this fight..."

"Tell me while I pace."

"Stop."

"Can't."

"Sit down before I knock you down."

The barely audible growl halted Arthur in his tracks. He sat down next to Bedwyr.

"We've sparred with each other, but we've never fought side by side, eh?"

"Right."

"But you've trained with other men. You know how to fight in a pair." He looked at Arthur intently. "You have to remember your training. Don't go in recklessly. Keep your head about you."

"I will."

"And use your right hand."

Without thinking, Arthur chuckled suggestively. "I usually do."

Bedwyr glared at him.

Arthur swallowed his mirth. "Should I take up on your right or left?"

"My right."

Desperate to lighten the situation, Arthur winked. "So our swords don't tangle?"

Bedwyr leaned into him, but his expression was hard as stone. "Watch your words," he murmured.

Chastened, Arthur nodded. "How about I just cover your right-hand side?"

"There's an idea."

Arthur was quiet for a while, listening to the other men beginning to snore. The sound only drew the muscles in Arthur's back more taut. Taking a chance, he pressed his shoulder into Bedwyr's. "Feel good about your left arm?" he asked softly.

Bedwyr was staring straight ahead into the darkness of the forest. Arthur thought he wouldn't answer, but then he said, "I do." He glanced sideways, though not far enough to meet Arthur's eyes. "You should try to sleep. I'll wake you."

He knew Bedwyr well enough to know he was finished talking for the time being. He probably wanted to prepare his mind for the work ahead. Easing onto the ground, Arthur settled with his back against the log and closed his eyes.

He listened to the sounds of the winter night and thought about the man next to him. Bedwyr had survived a warrior-ending injury, and now Arthur was determined Bed would not only survive the skirmish ahead but show every fighting man he was still one of them.

Shielded by the night, he slipped an arm behind Bedwyr's leg and curled his hand around the solid ankle of his boot. A few seconds later, the air stirred as Bedwyr's cloak settled around Arthur's shoulders.

He stroked the leather under his thumb and sank into sleep.

CHAPTER 18

As Arthur dozed, his question rang in Bedwyr's mind.

He was doubting his left arm and every decision he'd made since Arthur had appeared at the hut with word of the Saxons. But he'd kept his uncertainty to himself. He probably didn't belong here, but Arthur did. Though neither of his parents carried a weapon, the cub had been born to this, born for it—he was too strong, too agile, too fucking fearless for anyone to think otherwise. Battle would be where Arthur made his name and his mark, but only if he gained experience. At least Bedwyr could take some small measure of satisfaction in having helped him in that.

Kept awake by the discomfort of the shield harness, he thought about the fight ahead. He ran every possible opponent through his mind—how they would strike, how he'd block, when he'd use his sword and when his shield. He would keep to Arthur's left and guard his back when necessary. He was used to shielding a tall companion in Cai, though he hadn't felt quite this responsibility since their earliest skirmishes.

He looked down at Arthur's hair, at its strangely prim queue and moon-dulled colors. Who was Bedwyr trying to fool? Not the gods, nor himself. Even with Cai he'd never felt this responsibility. The imperative gripping him now went far beyond anything so limited as obligation or discipline. Master Matthias said he'd been protecting Arthur for years, and he supposed that was true. But this was a greater thing, what he felt looking at the curve of Arthur's head, feeling the heavy warmth of his hand on his boot.

He would kill anyone who came near Arthur. He only wished this fight to come wouldn't be his last chance to do so.

"You're ready?" His father's voice came through the dark like a distant rock slide.

Bedwyr looked up to see the broad shape of him against the stars. He had watched Uthyr closely in the armory, seeking any hint of his opinion of his presence here, but his father wore a mask well. He could learn from that too, he supposed. "Yes."

Uthyr looked at where Arthur slumped against the log.

Bedwyr pushed his foot forward so that Arthur's hand slid off.

His father didn't seem to notice. "Is he ready?"

"Yes."

Uthyr grunted. "His mother gave me a scorching earful when you left the smithy the other night. If anything happens to him, she'll have my sac."

Now that was something he wished he'd witnessed. He half smiled, imagining it, then realized his father had just shared something he needn't have shared. Rattled, he managed only, "He's a grown man."

"No lad is a man in his mother's eyes."

He wouldn't know. His mother had died before his fourth year. "Nothing will happen to him."

His father looked at him long enough that he was glad his shield hid his stump.

"Make sure of it," Uthyr said, then strode away.

Bedwyr stared at the receding bulk of his father. His instinct to protect Arthur had transformed into something with hard edges, implacable and undeniable. But for Uthyr to order it...

Was it only Uthyr's self-protective instinct to avoid Mistress Britte's wrath? Or could it be a sign he believed he could trust Bedwyr to keep Arthur safe, to shield him as capably as any other warrior?

And would he give Bedwyr more opportunities to do so?

Hope raised the small hairs on the back of his neck, as if tiny scales were pushing through his skin, spreading inch by inch to become his dragon's armor. Under cover of his cloak, he set a hand on Arthur's shoulder. Then he sat on the log, watching the steam of his breath rise in the night, eager now to turn it to fire.

~

It was odd to kneel next to someone other than Cai. Bedwyr and Cai each had their pre-battle rituals and had always gone about them quietly and separately. Arthur didn't seem to do anything special, and Bedwyr wondered if he ought to mention the value of such a thing. He could feel the cub's anticipation jittering from his body as keenly as if they lay naked and tangled. The thought drew something taut in his middle, and he wished he could touch Arthur. But his nearest shoulder and elbow were strapped into his shield, and they were surrounded by other men besides.

"Which one?" Arthur said, voice as low as the light.

Bedwyr found him watching the Saxon camp intently. "What?"

"Which man?" Arthur turned to him. "Cai says you choose one."

"Ah." Another reminder of their newness to each other. He nodded to the camp. "Second fire from the left, big lump on this side."

"Yeah?"

"Lying on his back, and his armor's out of easy reach. He'll be slower than most."

"Got it."

Bedwyr studied Arthur's profile, set in determination. He could almost hear the cub telling himself, over and over, that he wouldn't fail this time. "You won't."

Arthur turned, frowning, and Bedwyr shook his head.

"Just stay with me."

"Not behind you."

"No, at my side."

The frown eased. Arthur's gaze flicked briefly to Bedwyr's mouth as if to confirm his words, then met his own again. "I will."

In the pre-dawn hush, the promise sounded a greater thing than Arthur surely meant it to be. Bedwyr knocked his shield lightly against Arthur's. "You'll have new ink tonight."

Arthur's lips curled up on one side. "Tempt the gods, why don't you?"

The words echoed, familiar, but Bedwyr couldn't recall why before Uthyr's signal sounded.

Chaos reigned among the invaders, but he and Arthur worked together like a well-greased hinge. Arthur stayed on his right, his shield overlapping Bedwyr's slightly, affording him more protection and allowing him to focus on his sword work.

Bedwyr spoke a near-constant stream of instruction and encouragement to his new shieldmate. It was strange to do so, when he and Cai had often fought in silence, so accustomed were they to each other's rhythms. It had allowed him to lose himself in the battle, trusting Cai to balance him.

Though that sort of single-minded focus had always given him a sense of extreme awareness, speaking to Arthur made him feel present to an extent he wasn't prepared for. He heard every strike, every grunt and shout, every shrill and gasping scream as an invader perished nearby. He sensed opponents nearing by the scent of their fear, or a vibration of the earth under his boot. At moments, his sword and Arthur's, and those of the men they clashed with, moved as if they stood on the bottom of a pond, swinging through water.

Throughout, he spoke to Arthur, and throughout, Arthur responded immediately and obediently.

Until a very large right-handed Saxon burst from the melee to Bedwyr's left.

He must have flinched because the raider grinned. With only a few strokes, he drove Bedwyr back several paces. Arthur stayed with him, guarding his right shoulder. His left was wearying quickly. A few blows later, the Saxon knocked his sword from his hand.

He had one bright, terrible moment when he feared his hand had been dispatched with his weapon.

But it was there, and then so was Arthur. Lunging to Bedwyr's newly exposed side, Arthur laid into the Saxon with a series of strikes that were blinding in their speed.

Bedwyr scrambled to pick up his sword.

Driving the man back, Arthur continued to deal the unpredictable blows, until the Saxon tried to sidestep. By then, Bedwyr had caught up to them. Planting one boot behind the Saxon's, he tripped him. The raider hit the ground hard. Before the man could recover control of his weapon, Arthur drove his sword home with a roar.

Bedwyr stared at him for an immeasurable moment, for the man beside him had become more than a man. Outwardly, he was Arthur—same hair, same eyes, same strong hands. But something in the lines of his face and arms, in the timbre of his voice...

If Bedwyr sensed a dragon in himself in these places where they spilled invaders' blood, here was the bear of Arthur's namesake. Fierce, powerful, and deadly when awakened from its slumber. Bedwyr could almost see it, as if Arthur were throwing its shadow behind him. Except that it inhabited his body too, so that he stood next to Bedwyr, every tooth and claw at the ready.

To Bedwyr's right, just as the great bear in the stars stood beside the dragon, as if those beasts in the night sky were shieldmates, and always had been.

With a grunt, Arthur pulled his sword free and took up his position again, shield overlapping Bedwyr's, and they and their men put down the rest of the invading force.

When the last Saxon fell, Bedwyr let his sword drop to his side. Glancing at Arthur, his greatest hope and worst fear was realized: the bear was there still, looking back at him intently so that every muscle in Bedwyr's body fought conflicting urges. One told him to run away; the other pushed him to step forward and risk a collision that might destroy everyone around them.

Bedwyr knew he wanted the collision. And he knew it couldn't happen here.

Keeping his body reined tightly, he scanned his shieldmate for injuries. Arthur's skin and clothes bore a fair spatter of blood and gore, but Arthur himself had suffered only a few scrapes. He stood tall and strong, a tested warrior, finally.

Intent on inspecting every scratch and bruise—later, in a much safer place—Bedwyr turned and walked away.

CHAPTER 19

The ink stung, but Arthur didn't care. As Dafydd worked beside him, pricking him almost continuously with his needle, Arthur watched the room.

The hall was jubilant with their victory. It was rare for him to be the still one, but the one who usually filled that role was being welcomed back into the fold, as he deserved to be. Once in a while, someone jostled Bedwyr's short arm, and Arthur caught the slight wince that crossed his features, but for the most part Bedwyr looked happier than he'd ever seen him. Granted, he was Bedwyr, so he wore the happiness with more reserve than anyone else in the hall, but it was there in the flush on his cheeks and the relaxed slump of his great shoulders.

Grandpapa Wolf had told him once that, barring all else, he should try to be the best friend he could be to Bedwyr, and the fiercest fighter—a man who would guard Bedwyr's back on the battlefield and at home. His grandfather had known what he harbored for his brother's best friend and, in retrospect, had done his best to prepare Arthur for disappointment.

He tried not to feel that disappointment now. He had taken his grandfather's advice, had pushed Bed until he could fight again. Then he'd fought beside him, and they'd been fierce. Saxon after Saxon had fallen to their swords. Before this skirmish, he'd only thought about himself in a fight—how he must face an opponent and bring him down. He'd trained alongside men in an imitation of shieldmate work, but it had never felt the way it had this time.

This time, it had been as if he and Bedwyr shared a mind. Shared a body, for that matter. At some point it had come to feel as if his arms were Bedwyr's to command. Only afterward had he realized Bedwyr *had* commanded his arms, that his voice had accompanied him through the entire bloody rout like a low, steady heartbeat.

He'd realized this because Bedwyr hadn't spoken another word to him since. When the last man fell, Bed had scanned Arthur from head to boot, checking for injuries presumably, and then given him a long, hard look. Arthur had stared at him, at the blood spattered on his face, and his throat had become thick with all the things he wanted to say at once. But he'd been too slow. After a silent nod, Bedwyr had wiped his blade clean and walked away. Cai had found Bed then, thumping him on the back, and then Lord Uthyr had done the same. Several men gave Arthur similar thumps, and Master Tiro had kept him company on the trek home. He hoped Tiro hadn't noticed how many times he must have looked at Bedwyr across the campfire.

As he was doing now. What had happened at the hut was probably a fluke. A product of loneliness, or frustration, or even just an instinct to stay warm. Now that Bedwyr would rejoin the community...

It hurt to think it, but it would do him no good to want what he couldn't have. The past several weeks were just that to Bedwyr—past—and Arthur would have to move on too. He would take his grandfather's advice. If he and Bedwyr continued to fight together, he would put his own life in the way of anyone bent on harming his shieldmate. And at home—

"That should do it," Dafydd said.

Arthur looked down at his right arm, where a proud dragon stood on its hind feet and clawed at his shoulder. "Thanks, Dafydd."

"You've waited long enough," the carpenter said wryly, packing away his ink and instrument.

Cai toasted the new ink with a wave of his mug that sloshed ale onto Arthur's bare chest. His sister Mora poked at the puffy skin under the figure, knowing it would hurt. His parents looked at the tattoo and then at each other in a way he couldn't interpret.

"Arthur ap Matthias!"

Lord Uthyr's booming voice silenced the hall.

Arthur turned to face him.

"Well, lad, let's see it."

His neighbors murmured as Arthur passed and they caught sight of his tattoo. When he stood before Uthyr, he showed him his arm.

Uthyr studied it, then gave him a look of challenge. "If I were a suspicious man, I'd think you were planning to overthrow me."

Arthur straightened. "No, my lord. Only to honor your house."

"I notice you didn't ask Dafydd to ink over your youthful indiscretion."

He hadn't. It remained on his other arm. "A man owns his mistakes, my lord."

Uthyr sat back, and a slow smile curved his mouth. "Well said. There's hope for you yet." He beckoned Arthur closer until he could speak into his ear. "I saw how you fought this morning. Someday soon there may be a place at my side...a place of great trust and authority."

Arthur swallowed. Wasn't that place meant for Bedwyr? "I don't know what to say."

"Don't say anything. Keep fighting. Keep growing. Keep impressing me." Uthyr pushed him away and grinned. "But tonight, grab a cup and drink to your victory."

Someone shoved a mug of ale into his hand and toasted it with their own. He mumbled the proper response, feeling disoriented. His eyes roved the room.

Bedwyr was watching him from the far side, where he stood among some of the other fighters. His expression was unreadable, and Arthur wondered if the tattoo had been a mistake. Eira came to stand next to Bedwyr, placing one hand on his belly and leaning close to whisper to him.

Arthur turned away. That was that. They would go back to normal. Bedwyr had to do it. Everyone ignored Masters Philip and Tiro, and their obvious devotion to each other, because they were old and silvered. His neighbors seemed to think that Tiro and his man couldn't possibly be getting up to anything anymore. Arthur knew from having lived with his grandfathers that desire and the follow-through on it didn't necessarily diminish with age. But that didn't matter if Bedwyr wasn't inclined to find out.

Besides, it was a grave risk, and Bed didn't take those off the battlefield.

Arthur took a sip from his cup, but it was sour and Uthyr's words rattled too loudly in his mind. He needed something constructive to do. Handing the ale to someone else, he made for the door.

The air outside felt cool and fresh against his face. After a few paces, he realized he'd forgotten his shirt, wadded and stuffed under the bench he'd sat on while Dafydd inked him. He would fetch it later. Going back into the humid reek of the hall held no appeal. Instead, he stopped in the smithy, where he gathered three sturdy hinges, several nails, and a hammer, and then he walked up the path to the shepherd's hut.

When he stepped inside, he paused for a moment to sniff the air. He could just make it out, the scent he'd come to associate with Bedwyr. He'd been surrounded by it when they'd shared the bed. If he were to cross to it now and press his nose into the bedding, it would be strong. But there was no sense in torturing himself.

After building a fire to warm and light the small space, he set about repairing the door. It was a simple job, and he admonished himself for not having done it sooner. When he'd driven home the final nail, he set the hammer on the table and eyed the door. It wasn't much, but it looked as it should now, and he wished he could present it to Bedwyr himself. But what would Bed want with this hut now that he could live in the village again? Shrugging off his silly thoughts, Arthur swung the door open to test the new hinges.

Bedwyr stood on the other side of the threshold, lit by the moon.

He held up a fistful of cloth. "You forgot your shirt."

Arthur stepped aside to let him in. After not being here with him for a few days, Bedwyr seemed to fill the place. The color was still high in his cheeks, from drink or the walk to the hut. Would his skin be warm or cool? Arthur wanted to touch it to find out.

"You repaired the door?"

"Yes."

Bedwyr tried the hinges a few times before closing the door and latching it. When he turned to Arthur, his gaze slipped down his chest. "It needs a good bolt, don't you think?"

Heat flashed across Arthur's shoulders, but he caught himself. The man was only stating a fact. He wanted his privacy now. "Um, I'll leave you to it. I'll ask my mother about a bolt. Tomorrow."

He moved to leave, but Bedwyr stepped in his path.

Arthur pulled up short.

"I have a few things to say."

"All right." He waited for Bedwyr to tick off the many reasons he shouldn't return to the hut, bolt in hand or no.

"Thank you."

Of course he would be polite about it. "Sure."

"I mean it," Bedwyr said, frowning. "For all of it. For helping me train. For convincing me to fight. For shielding me."

But not for the other moments, the desperate, grasping ones. "You forgot the hinges." A weak joke, but Bedwyr's words were the beginning of an ending.

An unexpected smile split his dark beard. "For the hinges." He set a hand to Arthur's shoulder, his expression sobering again. "I owe you a great debt."

There it was. He was practically opening the door and shooing Arthur out. Time for the cub to go back to his own den and forget this place. His freshly tattooed skin ached under Bedwyr's hand. His chest ached too. The dragon had been a mistake. "Anyone could have done it," he said, adding lamely, "I mean, they're hinges."

"Fuck the hinges."

Arthur took a startled step backward, and Bedwyr followed him.

"You don't want the burden of my gratitude. Just as I didn't want the burden of your guilt."

"That isn't why I came up here then," he said, then added, "Not the only reason." It seemed this was another place he couldn't speak lies.

"I know," Bedwyr said. "My father told you he'd banish you if you didn't succeed."

"Who told you that?"

"Your father."

When had his father—? It didn't matter. "I wanted to come, Bed. I wanted to help. I'm sorry I didn't tell you myself."

Bedwyr studied him intently. "Why didn't you?"

"I didn't want to admit I'd been a coward. That I'd needed your father's shove. Then I just thought...I had to do it on my own."

Bedwyr nodded. "Well, you did."

Right, it was time to leave. Arthur nodded back, unable to say anything.

But before he could move, Bedwyr jabbed at Arthur's breastbone with one blunt fingertip. "You," he said. "Only you." Bedwyr looked at him for a long moment, as if to make sure his words were understood. Then he pulled Arthur into a kiss.

Arthur leaned against him, tasting, noting, trying to store it all away in his mind. He filled his hands with as much of the man as he could get away with, sliding his palms down Bedwyr's back and onto his rump. As he kissed him back, he held on, memorizing the shape of him.

As goodbye kisses went, Bedwyr was giving him one to remember. Aggressive and lingering at the same time, with deep rumbles of satisfaction that were starting to send Arthur's blood to his cock. Before he could think thoughts that might prevent it, he was hard and pressing into Bed's hip. Then the warm weight of Bedwyr's hand covered one of his own, and Arthur kissed harder, knowing he was about to be removed from the premises.

But Bedwyr didn't remove him or his wayward hands. Instead, he caught Arthur's lower lip between his teeth. "Do you want to leave?"

Arthur shuddered. "No."

Bedwyr pulled away and shucked his belt and shirt. He did it naturally now, as though he'd never had a second hand, as though he had all the power he'd ever need in the body he now owned. He held his gnarled wrist before Arthur's face. "Still want to stay?"

"*Yes.*"

"Good. I have a few more things to say."

As Arthur stood rooted to the ground, Bedwyr shoved the table in front of the door. When he turned back, he looked almost like he had just before the battle, muscles coiled and brow drawn down with deadly focus.

Was this to be Arthur's reckoning? Should he be speaking to his gods, pleading for a final gift of good will?

He'd scarcely begun to think their names in his mind, when Bedwyr stepped toward him. Hooking a finger into Arthur's belt, he tugged, hard.

CHAPTER 20

Arthur took the hint and unfastened it, letting it fall to the floor. Bedwyr was already lifting the hem of his shirt; Arthur peeled it up and off his arms. That big, warm hand smoothed down his chest, thumb teasing a nipple, and gooseflesh spread over Arthur's skin. Bedwyr pulled him to the bed and lay down.

"Straddle me."

Gods.

Laid out below him, the man was substantial, taking up the width of the bed with his massive shoulders and arms, so that Arthur wondered how he had ever fit on the same mattress. He smoothed his hands over the muscle of Bedwyr's chest, pushed his fingers through the thick, dark hair that grew down his torso. This body, this hair, was so different from his own. He bent to taste, curling his tongue over salty skin before using the tip to flick a nipple.

Bedwyr grunted.

Arthur's cock grew heavier at the sound. He dragged his lips to the other nipple and flicked his tongue again, hard. Bedwyr took hold of his head, but when Arthur thought he would hold him fast to his chest, Bedwyr raised him instead. He was frowning.

"Not like that."

"Not like what?"

"Rough. I don't want it rough."

"What do you want?"

"I want…" But Bedwyr's voice trailed off into gruff silence. For the first time since he'd entered the hut, he seemed to have run out of words.

"Whatever it is…" Arthur cringed at how desperate he sounded.

But Bedwyr only picked up Arthur's hand and set it on his chest. Holding his gaze, Bedwyr stroked the back of it with a soft touch.

"You want it gentle?"

Bedwyr's dark brows drew together, as if he didn't like admitting it.

Warmth bloomed in Arthur's middle. Bending again, he brushed his lips over Bed's nipple, then up his chest and throat to his mouth. "I can do that. Trust me?"

A rush of hot breath was his answer.

He slid down Bedwyr's body. When the man reached for his laces, Arthur stayed his hand. He looked up, asked the silent question.

Bedwyr licked his lip and let his hand fall to the mattress.

Arthur plucked at the lacing of his trousers. When they lay open, Arthur did the same for his boots and pulled everything down and off his body. He dispatched his own as well, then feasted on the sight before him, making a more deliberate survey. Powerful shoulders, broad chest. A thick torso into sturdy hips. Heavy, muscular thighs bracing his own. Bedwyr's skin bore several scars from skirmishes, and Arthur wanted to ask him about each one. In the flicker of the firelight, Bedwyr's tattoos seemed to breathe with life, to dance and beckon. Arthur began to trail his fingertips over them, as lightly as he could.

A low groan grated from Bed's throat.

Arthur skimmed up his ribs and over his collarbones. Across his shoulders and down his arms. Along his sides and inward toward his navel. He kept his fingers light, using only the sensitive tips. The effect was one he never would have expected: the gentler he was, the harsher Bedwyr's breaths became.

By the time Arthur neared his cock, Bedwyr was watching his hands with wide eyes. Arthur eased his fingers up the thick shaft. Slowly, he pulled the foreskin down to expose the head. When he blew a puff of air across it, Bedwyr came alive under him, hips bucking.

"Yeah?"

"Yeah." Bed sounded choked.

Arthur wanted to hear him crack and fall apart.

The hair at Bedwyr's crotch was even thicker than that on his chest. In the firelight, it looked glossy. Leaning down, he pressed his nose into it and inhaled.

There was the scent, the stronger, more pungent version of what permeated the bedding. It was what he'd expected to find—sweat and musk—but there was an eager warmth behind it that transformed it into something more. Something only Bedwyr had, and something only Arthur could find. He slipped a hand under his prick again. "Heavy," he said, glancing up to a dark-eyed stare. He took it in his mouth.

He'd tried to imagine what this would be like, but it turned out that having a cock in his mouth wasn't something he could have prepared for. Not really. It felt even thicker than it was, and it tasted tangy and sort of bitter. It pushed of its own will against the roof of his mouth. Slowly, he tried to swallow it.

Bedwyr flinched, and Arthur gagged.

Coughing, he pulled up to eye his quarry. It was just a cock. He'd watched Eira do this, and she was half his size…

He stilled, thinking about that night, about how vigorously Eira had worked, the hard curve of her wrist and the force with which she'd tugged.

And how Bedwyr had gripped the woodpile and stared past her.

Gently, he wrapped a hand around the base of Bedwyr's cock. He kissed up the shaft, then brushed down it again, until the tender skin and wiry hair had set his lips tingling. He circled the cockhead with his tongue and slipped it into his mouth, sucking lightly.

Bedwyr groaned, long and loud. His knees pressed into Arthur's sides. "Again."

He stroked the dusky skin, but softly, tasting and nuzzling, and Bedwyr's thighs had him trapped. Fingers slipped into his hair and pulled, just a bit.

"Yes."

He kept at it, stroking with a hand while he sucked and nibbled. Bedwyr didn't speak to him, as he had on the battlefield, but his hand joined Arthur's in the stroking, showing him what he wanted before falling away to grab the blankets. Gradually his moans grew louder and his hips began to push off the mattress.

Arthur had never sucked a prick before, but he could guess when a man was about to spend, and when Bedwyr's legs shook with the effort to thrust into Arthur's mouth, he let him, holding his breath and blinking past the urge to gag, until he tasted Bed's seed.

~ ~ ~

Bedwyr lay for a moment, watching the rafters shift against the thatching in the firelight. As they flickered, he grew aware of Arthur's weight on his legs. Reaching down, he dragged him up until he could take his mouth. Arthur groaned into him so that his own chest seemed to reverberate with the sound. Bedwyr held him hard, almost overwhelmed by a desire to give him anything. Give him everything.

He broke away. "What do you want?"

Arthur gave him a dazed look. "Your hand. Wet."

He helped Arthur straddle him again. His cub's cock stood high, his sac drawn up tight underneath. Spitting into his hand, Bedwyr wrapped him up. He crooked his other arm behind Arthur's arse, bracing him close.

"Hard and fast," Arthur murmured.

That much he'd learned over the past few days. He'd used it to subjugate this man, keep him bound up in his own pleasure so he wouldn't force Bedwyr to admit his wants. But now that he wanted to get it just right—make it as good as what Arthur had given him—setting a rhythm was proving more difficult than he'd expected. He gritted his teeth, biting back his frustration. "Sorry, it's my weak hand."

Arthur leaned down and nipped his ear. "There's nothing weak about that hand," he said. "Fuck me."

Bedwyr growled, determined, and spit into his palm again. Arthur straightened, watching him. Setting his hands on Bedwyr's thighs, he pushed into his fist. In the firelight, the flat planes of his body twisted as he moved. Arthur felt right sitting astride him, grinding against his belly, and Bedwyr felt foolish for not letting him have this advantage sooner. He wanted his cub in every way he could imagine, but this…being able to see every sinew flex and stretch…

More, though, he wanted to be just where he was. Taking Arthur's weight, holding him up, giving him the space and shelter to become this man who was emerging—it gave him an absurd pride. He had no claim on Arthur's strength or his courage, or on any of the vulnerable parts of his body that this angle made plain.

But the pride was fierce nevertheless, and hungry. Gripping

Arthur more tightly, he didn't let up until the cub's thighs trembled with the effort to support him. He came with a force that arched his spine and filled the hut with a harsh shout.

He sat for a moment, his ribs contracting on strained breaths. Bedwyr smoothed his hand up Arthur's belly to feel them rise and fall. Arthur looked down at him, then collapsed onto his hands over Bedwyr and grinned. "Thanks."

Bedwyr laughed and tugged him down to lie on his chest. Arthur sprawled on top of him for a few minutes, letting Bedwyr get his arms' fill. He closed his eyes, a deep sense of contentment spreading through him. Of all the times he'd imagined being with another man, he'd only imagined grinding friction and the chase to release. He'd not foreseen this moment of sated silence, of living strength breathing against him. This is what the striving earned. He tightened his hold on Arthur, pushing his face into his cub's neck. Arthur shifted to nuzzle him back, before sliding off.

Bedwyr rolled to face him. He looked much as he had after the skirmish—eyes sharp and color high. Bedwyr reached behind Arthur's head and slipped free the cord that bound his hair. He sifted his fingers through it. "Why do you keep it tied?"

"What do you mean?"

Bedwyr shrugged. "Seems you'd want to show it off."

Arthur smiled. "Why?"

"Are you joking?"

"Are you?"

Bedwyr shook his head. "If I had your hair, I'd show it off."

Arthur's teeth flashed as he grinned. "No, you wouldn't."

The grin was catching. "Fair enough. But why don't you?"

"My grandfather."

"Marcus?"

"No, Wolf. I spent a lot of time in the smithy, needing *direction*..."

Bedwyr chuckled. He could only imagine.

"He made me tie it. Hazard otherwise."

"I have to agree with him there."

Arthur's eyes flicked between his own, and he blinked. "You like it loose?"

"Yes." It felt good to admit it.

Even better when Arthur didn't tease him for it.

He slid his fingers down to trace Arthur's new ink, a dragon that reached for his shoulder. When he'd seen it in the hall, heat had flashed over his skin, as if the beast had aimed its fiery breath at him. "You told my father you honored his house."

"That's what I told him."

"Is it true?"

"In a way."

He studied Arthur's expression, but it was calmly blank.

Finally, Arthur said, "You're of his house too."

Once again, he was enveloped in warmth. It radiated from his fool's heart up to his scalp and out along each limb. He used one tingling finger to trace the tattoo. "It's a good dragon."

"Better than the first one."

He stopped his tracing and glanced up, surprised. "Cai said that was a dog."

"Cai's an idiot."

And so, maybe, was Bedwyr. "You told Uthyr you kept it to remember your mistakes."

"That's what I told him."

"Lying to a warlord is a dangerous game."

"So is this."

Bedwyr's chest rose and fell on a truth he couldn't keep to himself. "It's not a game to me."

Arthur laid a hand to his skin, must have felt the thump of Bedwyr's heart against his palm. "It's never been a game to me." Arthur smiled. "You know how your dagger is just like Cai's?"

The blades had similar shapes and each bore a letter for its owner's name. "Yes?"

"It wasn't when I designed it."

"I thought Master Wolf only said that to include you—about the designing."

Arthur shook his head and gave an embarrassed laugh. "The final designs were more his doing, yes. Because when I first drew them up, yours was much larger." He looked up to meet Bedwyr's eyes. "And it had a dragon on it."

At that, Bedwyr felt a fondness for the lads they had been. "Should've made that one."

"Grandpapa thought it would show up Cai, so he talked me into identical blades." He touched the ink on Bedwyr's arm. "I couldn't let go of the notion, though, of giving you a dragon."

Gods. "So you put one on yourself."

"Twice now." Arthur drew a breath against him. "I kept the old tattoo because it isn't mine to cover, Bed. It belongs to you. It marked the beginning."

"Of this?"

"Of this."

"What is this?"

Arthur's long fingers pushed into Bedwyr's hair, cupping the back of his head. "I don't know." He tightened his grip. "It's not guilt."

"Nor gratitude," Bedwyr blurted, then added, "Mostly." He acknowledged Arthur's smile. But it brought out everything young and reckless in the cub's face, and the old protectiveness surged up. "We have to take care."

"I know."

Gods' blood, what were they thinking? It was one thing to take advantage of an empty hut. What would they do as winter became spring? As they tried to move about their lives among other people again? As they fought side by side, each of their beasts drawing out the other? "I don't know what the fuck I'm doing."

Arthur laughed softly against him. "And I do?" He studied Bedwyr, but for once it didn't make him want to retreat into himself. "Maybe you keep me from doing foolish things sometimes. Maybe I push you now and then to act before you can overthink. It's a balance, like a well-crafted sword."

"That's...poetic." He teased, but the words calmed him. He'd never thought to get that from this man.

"I speak the language of my grandfathers." Arthur leaned in and knocked their foreheads together lightly. "So do you."

So he did. *Ddraig* to *ddraig*, each man in his line had taught the next to fight, to survive. So had Arthur's ancestors. Bedwyr slid his fingers into Arthur's hair again and kissed him, slow and deep. "So we're their legacy?"

Arthur's eyes seemed to dance in the light from the hearth. "We are."

They were.

Bedwyr whistled low. "May the gods protect us from ourselves."

EPILOGUE

Arthur woke early to the cry of a falcon in the valley.

Bedwyr lay behind him, his chest pressing against Arthur's back on the relaxed, shallow breaths of deep sleep. As always, one arm lay over Arthur's waist, its fingers in a loose curl before his belly. His head rested on Bed's short arm.

He studied it for some time, that arm that should have been complete. But it wasn't and never would be. One mistake had cost Bedwyr the future he'd thought he had.

Arthur thought about his grandfather and his long-ago advice. Be a friend, he'd said, on the battlefield and at home.

He eased from the bunk and dressed. One more glance at Bedwyr to give him the courage he needed, and then he slipped from the hut quietly.

The world outside lay still, no sign of the falcon that had woken him. The rising sun shone between the mountainous horizon and the woolly sky like a blade just drawn from the fire pan, giving the snow all around him a reddish glow. A fresh layer had fallen overnight, obscuring the two sets of footprints leading to the hut. He followed them to the path, around the broad hill, and into the village.

He found the man he sought in the armory, as he knew he would.

"Lord Uthyr."

Dark eyes flashed up from the sword he was honing. They were so like Bedwyr's...yet not. "You're up early. Didn't you celebrate?"

"Had my share of ale." He scanned the armor hanging from its hooks, always ready. "I hoped to speak with you."

"About?"

With a deep breath, he approached his commander. "The things you said last night. About trust and authority."

Uthyr set down the blade and whetstone. "You've given my words some thought?"

"Yes."

"And?"

An invisible cord tightened around his body and pulled, out of the armory and up the path to a small, warm hut and the man sleeping inside it, unaware. What would Bed do if he knew Arthur stood here now, about to say something that could change both their futures? Would it matter to him that Arthur was doing it for him?

On the battlefield and at home.

He spoke before the unseen cord could snap.

"I'll make you proud," he said. "I'll make myself worthy of your trust."

Uthyr looked at him for a long, agonizing moment. Then he smiled.

It made his eyes shine like a crow's.

"I know you will, Arthur." He gripped Arthur's arm in one great, scarred hand and squeezed, sending a sharp ache through the new ink. "You're the son I didn't have."

Arthur wished the ground would open and swallow him.

It didn't.

So he stood, bearing the weight of those black eyes, until Uthyr picked up the sword again and scraped the whetstone down its edge.

AUTHOR'S NOTE

A funny thing happens when you decide to write your own version of a beloved legend: you might feel the need to post flashing WARNING signs.

When I was still on Twitter, I posted something like, "What you won't find in *Sons of Britain*: knights, magic, grail quests, tournaments, damsels in distress." Because reader expectations are huge in genre fiction, and I planned to ignore some very specific expectations surrounding Arthurian legend. How dare!

So why dare, or even bother? Simple: it's a rich legend with lots of room for interpretation and origin stories. I had two main goals for *Sons of Britain*: to write a version of Arthur's story that was more realistic than fantastical, and to create a story someone could read and then think, "I can see how those characters and events could—over centuries—become the legend we know."

To give the story a realistic feel, I set it in 6th-Century Britain. The earliest mentions of Arthur came from what is now Cymru/Wales. It made sense to me that Arthur might be raised in a mountainous region, so the early books are set in the area now known as Eryri/Snowdonia. Knights didn't exist in post-Roman Britain, but a man living in that time period and place might be trained as a warrior by necessity, to defend his land from the tide of settlers from the Continent. Ideals of chivalry and courtly love came to the legend later in the middle ages. In the so-called Dark Ages, survival was a much higher priority than ivory-tower behavior. So this Arthur is a warrior, living and fighting under a warlord's authority.

Which brings me to my second goal. "Wasn't Uthyr Arthur's father?" you might ask. In many accounts, yes, and among the accounts we know best, almost always. But I wanted the freedom to take a different approach. To do so, I decided to use the spirit of the legend, not the letter of it. So my Uthyr isn't Arthur's father, but he fulfills much of that kind of role: he's the ultimate authority in Arthur's world, he trains Arthur to his vocation, Arthur looks to him for validation and, eventually, will be faced with the prospect of leading people in a way similar to Uthyr's leadership.

"But wait, wait, wait," you say. "What about Uthyr and Igraine? That's in everything!"

To me, the most important thing about that part of the legend is that Uthyr felt something toward the woman who became Arthur's mother, and those feelings made him do extraordinary and questionable things. And I will explore that story in this series. In fact, it'll have its own book down the line. *is coy*

So I've taken some liberties. (<<<understatement) Among them: my Arthur was raised by his birth parents, not fostered; Cai is his biological brother; Gwen is Uthyr's daughter; Bedwyr is Uthyr's son; the Myrddin (Merlin) is a titled role in society, not a name; and Lancelot...well, that's an author's note for a future book. *is coy again*

Of course, *Sons of Britain* explores another big thing I haven't mentioned yet: queer relationships among Arthurian characters. Many scholars agree that hints of queerness exist in the legend; one story they point to often is *Gawain and the Green Knight*, in which Gawain must give to Sir Bertilak anything he receives over a three-day period, including a succession of kisses from Bertilak's flirty wife. The queerness in the larger legend has been explored here and there by modern authors. But I saw an opportunity to merge two things: relationships on the queer spectrum and the bonds that develop between and among fighting men. These two ideas will come together strongly later in the series, when Arthur begins to gather trusted warriors around him.

Finally, a few words about Bedwyr...

Man, has this guy gotten short shrift in legend, especially after Lancelot was introduced in the 12th Century (upstart latecomer!). By that time, Bedwyr had become Sir Bedivere. But in the earliest Welsh tales, he was Bedwyr, Arthur's most trusted fellow warrior, a good friend of Cai's, notably good-looking, and very loyal. He was also often portrayed as having one hand or one arm. I've kept all of these traits because *yowza*, what a lot of opportunity for conflict. Though *Marked by Fire* introduces my version of the story, giving readers a new Arthur, I'd argue that this is very much Bedwyr's book. To my mind, the changes he has to undergo are the greater ones and ultimately require courage on a level no other character in the book must show. And who doesn't love a strong, quiet guy?

So Bedwyr will get his due in this series, along with characters you may be more familiar with, including Gwen, Cai, Gawain, Agravain, Palamedes, Uthyr, Merlin, and even Lancelot (sort of).

I hope you enjoy this new take on an old but loved story.

~ Mia

ACKNOWLEDGMENTS

Big thanks to editor Deborah Nemeth for her work on this book and her advice for the shape of the series to come. It's a blast to work with someone as pumped about Arthurian legend as I am.

Many thanks to Suzie D for sharing research into limb amputation and related recovery.

Thanks always to my husband, D, for giving me the time and space to write, and extra heart when I need it.

And thank you to the anonymous many who passed down legends of Arthur and Bedwyr over fires and ale, recorded a few of them, and then protected those fragile bits of paper, so that we, now, can have a taste of how the tales began.

THANK YOU!

Thank you for reading *Marked by Fire*!

Don't miss *Bound by Blood*,
the next book in the *Sons of Britain* series.

Learn about all new releases via Mia's email newsletter:

http://eepurl.com/LtFAf

(case-sensitive link)

ALSO BY MIA

The **STORM'S EDGE** Saga
Historical LGBTQ+

Into the Fire Series
Thrust
Strike
Forge
Quench
Hone
Fracture
Weld
Grind
Burnish

Sons of Britain Series
Marked by Fire
Bound by Blood
Driven by Duty
…and more to come!

ABOUT THE AUTHOR

Mia West strikes rough heroes against each other until they spark. She writes historical romance, with occasional forays into paranormal and contemporary. When not writing, Mia loves to read, hike, and travel. Super powers include parallel parking and map reading. She takes her wine red, her whisky rye, and her brownie from the middle of the pan.

Discover more at miawest.com

Made in the USA
San Bernardino, CA
18 September 2017